P9-DNN-038

The door handle began to move.

Lexie lifted the knife, prepared to bring it down on whatever part of Lanier's body came through the door.

Suddenly the handle stopped turning and the shadow moved away.

He was leaving? Why? Then a dog barked and she knew Chris and Teddy were close by.

"Lexie!" Hearing Chris shout her name made her close her eyes and thank God for sending him to her rescue.

"Lexie?" Chris's voice sounded as if he was in one of the bedrooms. "Are you okay?"

Rocky Mountain K-9 Unit

*These police officers fight for justice
with the help of their brave canine partners.*

Laura Scott has always loved romance and read faith-based books by Grace Livingston Hill in her teenage years. She's thrilled to have been given the opportunity to retire from thirty-eight years of nursing to become a full-time author. Laura has published over thirty books for Love Inspired Suspense. She has two adult children and lives in Milwaukee, Wisconsin, with her husband of thirty-five years. Please visit Laura at laurascottbooks.com, as she loves to hear from her readers.

Books by Laura Scott

Love Inspired Suspense

Rocky Mountain K-9 Unit

Hiding in Montana

Justice Seekers

Soldier's Christmas Secrets
Guarded by the Soldier
Wyoming Mountain Escape
Hiding His Holiday Witness
Rocky Mountain Standoff
Fugitive Hunt

Visit the Author Profile page at LoveInspired.com for more titles.

HIDING IN MONTANA

LAURA SCOTT

LOVE INSPIRED SUSPENSE
INSPIRATIONAL ROMANCE

If you purchased this book without a cover you should be aware that this book is stolen property. It was reported as "unsold and destroyed" to the publisher, and neither the author nor the publisher has received any payment for this "stripped book."

Special thanks and acknowledgment are given to Laura Scott for her contribution to the Rocky Mountain K-9 Unit miniseries.

LOVE INSPIRED® SUSPENSE
INSPIRATIONAL ROMANCE

Recycling programs
for this product may
not exist in your area.

ISBN-13: 978-1-335-55503-8

Hiding in Montana

Copyright © 2022 by Harlequin Enterprises ULC

All rights reserved. No part of this book may be used or reproduced in any manner whatsoever without written permission except in the case of brief quotations embodied in critical articles and reviews.

This is a work of fiction. Names, characters, places and incidents are either the product of the author's imagination or are used fictitiously. Any resemblance to actual persons, living or dead, businesses, companies, events or locales is entirely coincidental.

For questions and comments about the quality of this book, please contact us at CustomerService@Harlequin.com.

Love Inspired
22 Adelaide St. West, 41st Floor
Toronto, Ontario M5H 4E3, Canada
www.LoveInspired.com

Printed in U.S.A.

But he answered and said, It is written,
Man shall not live by bread alone, but by every word
that proceedeth out of the mouth of God.
—*Matthew* 4:4

This book is dedicated to my good friend Kathy Zdanowski. Your turn is coming, my friend. Don't give up. Keep writing!

ONE

Pilot Lexie McDaniels sat in her tiny corner office in the Blue Skye Aviation hangar and waited for the storm-tracking software to load on the computer screen. She had a flight tour scheduled the following morning and wanted to make sure the weather forecast hadn't changed. Living a few miles outside Great Falls, Montana, nestled in a valley between the Rocky Mountains, she knew from personal experience the conditions, especially the wind, could change on a dime.

A flash of movement through the window at her right caught her eye. She frowned and leaned forward to peer through the glass, attempting to pierce the darkness beyond. At nine o'clock at night, she was alone in the hangar. Skip the mechanic and Harry the airstrip owner had left hours ago.

She didn't see anything unusual. The light from the nearly full moon was partially obliterated by tall leafy trees lining the northwest corner of the parking lot. The runway was located in the opposite direction. Lexie frowned again and told herself she was imagining things. Still, her plane was her only way of supporting herself, so she rose and headed through the dark hangar, intending to go outside to check things out.

Most likely the wind had blown something past her window. There was no reason to worry. Five years ago, she'd put her past behind her. She was safe in Montana, as far from the big city of New York as a person could get.

Upon reaching the door, she wrinkled her nose at the horrible smell of body odor mixed with cigarette smoke mere seconds before hard hands grasped her shoulders, yanking her backward against a taut sweaty body.

"If you scream, you'll die." Hot smelly air hit her face.

No! The harsh words filled her with fear, but sheer survival instincts quickly kicked in. Lexie elbowed her attacker, stomped on his feet, but then went still as she felt the hard barrel of a gun dig painfully into her side.

"Stop it!" The man's grip tightened painfully. "Behave and you won't get hurt."

She had to swallow hard against the ball of fear lodged in her throat. She sent up a silent prayer for God to protect and guide her. "W-what do you want?"

"You." The single word was followed by a creepy laugh. Visions of being attacked or worse tumbled through her mind. "And that plane."

Her Cessna? Lexie instinctively dug in her heels. No way. Not happening.

But her assailant was strong and easily dragged her across the concrete floor of the hangar. She tried not to panic. To not think about the danger of flying at night in the mountains.

Yet what did that matter, anyway? This guy could very well kill her once her usefulness as a pilot was over.

"Wait!" The word came out hoarse as his arm was wrapped tightly around her neck, partially cutting off her air supply. "I need to have a mechanic check the plane before we go." She stalled for time; why exactly, she wasn't sure. "It's important the engine is in peak flying condition, especially if we're heading out at night."

"Nice try, but I saw you flying the plane earlier. It's fine. We're leaving. Now!" He ruthlessly dragged her forward.

Lord, please help me! She went limp, her sneakered feet dragging behind in a way that managed to tangle her legs with his.

It was enough to knock the sweaty guy off-balance. The arm around her throat loosened and the gun moved away from her side for a fraction of a second. She gathered her strength, but before she could react, the assailant abruptly let her go.

Lexie fell to the floor, her knees hitting the concrete hard, but then she quickly jumped up. She heard muffled grunts and saw two dark shadows fighting. A low growl had her taking several steps backward in fear. Through the darkness, she saw the whites of an animal's eyes.

What was going on? Suddenly one of the men groaned and slumped to the floor while the other jumped up and raced out of the hangar. The dog continued to bark and growl, giving chase to a point, but then stopping near the open hangar doorway. The dog wheeled around and ran back to the man on the floor.

Lexie felt certain the man who reeked of body odor was the one who'd disappeared outside, but the news wasn't entirely reassuring. What if this guy was an accomplice?

She edged around the stranger sprawled on the floor, giving the dog a wide berth as she made her way toward the light switch. The incandescent lights came on low at first, providing her eyes time to adjust as they slowly grew brighter.

The man on the floor didn't move. Was he dead? Was he involved with the man with the gun? She was torn between taking off and staying to make sure the stranger was alive. The dog sat right at his side, which made it impossible for her to approach.

"Good doggy" she said in a weak voice. "Nice doggy. Don't bite me, okay?"

The dog licked the stranger's face. The man let out a low moan, and finally lifted his head. "W-what happened?"

"You tell me." Lexie eyed him warily. "Who are you? What are you doing here?"

The man managed to sit up. He stroked the dog, calming the animal. "Ma'am, are you okay?"

"I'm not the one on the floor," she pointed out.

"Yeah." He put a hand to his head for a moment, then staggered to his feet. She noticed he had a backpack with him, yet he didn't seem like a hiker who'd wandered in. He was a bit unsteady as he stood there, looking around. Finally, he met her gaze. "I'm Chris Fuller, with the Rocky Mountain K-9 Unit." He shifted the backpack and lightly rested his hand on the dog's head. "And this is Teddy, my partner."

Lexie loved dogs, but nothing about this scenario was normal. Now that the animal had stopped growling, the brown-and-white spaniel appeared friendly enough. She crossed her arms over her chest, chilled despite the mild June temperatures. Finding two strangers in her hangar, in the span of a few minutes, was frightening.

Chris Fuller was well over six feet tall and wore casual black jeans paired with a black T-shirt covered with a bulky black vest. His warm brown skin highlighted his muscular arms and shoulders. He wore his black hair short and had a jagged scar over his left eyebrow, and his intense topaz gaze seemed to look right through her.

It took a moment to notice the blood on his temple. "You're hurt. I have a first-aid kit in my office."

"Not now." He waved his hand impatiently. "Do you know the man who attacked you?"

She shivered and shook her head. "No. Why? Is that why you're here?"

"Yeah." He frowned. "How long was I out?"

"Not long, less than a minute." She instinctively took a step backward as he approached. "Wait, how do I know you are who you say you are?"

He looked surprised by her question. He looked down at the front of his vest, then pulled the lanyard out from beneath to show her his badge. "I'm a cop, and so is Teddy. See his K-9 vest? You're safe with us. What's your name?"

"Alexandra McDaniels. I go by Lexie." She let out a relieved sigh. God had sent one of the good guys to save her. "Okay, I believe you and Teddy are cops, but why are you here?"

"We're tracking an escaped convict wanted for murder." The officer pulled paperwork from his back pocket and unfolded it. "Do you recognize this man? His name is Frank Lanier. Is he the person who attacked you?"

Lexie stared at the mug shot. There was something about his face that niggled at the back of her mind. Had she seen him on the news? "No, I can't say for sure. I'm sorry. It was dark, and he grabbed me from behind." The memory of the attack made her shiver again. "You believe this escaped convict is the man who attacked me? It would explain why he dragged me toward the plane and ordered me to fly him out of here."

If not for the officer and his dog showing up when they did, she might very well be up in the air right now with a brutal killer.

He must have seen the revulsion on her features. "Hey, it's okay." Chris's smile was reassuring. "You're safe, remember? Teddy tracked Frank Lanier here, and my partner is rarely wrong." He gave his dog another pat. "Don't worry, we'll find him and soon. Trust me, it's our job to make sure secrets don't stay buried for long."

Lexie stared at him, having trouble meeting his all-too-knowing topaz gaze. His statement about uncovering secrets struck a chord deep within.

Because it was imperative that *her* secrets remained hidden, forever.

Chris did his best to ignore the throbbing pain reverberating through his head. It irked him that Lanier had gotten away. He needed to get out there and find him, but not until he made certain Lexie was doing okay.

The pilot was stunningly beautiful, with long wavy dark hair and bright green eyes. She looked unnerved, and he felt bad for what she'd been through. Nothing bothered him more than men who mistreated women. "Lexie, why don't you let me escort you home? Teddy and I need to get back to tracking this guy as soon as possible."

"Just go. I'll be fine." Her attempt at a smile was pathetic. "Although I still think you should let me bandage your cut."

"I'd rather make sure you get home safely. My injury isn't serious." He'd suffered far worse as a risk-taking teen and in his career as a cop. After working for three years as a K-9 officer in Phoenix, Arizona, he'd been grateful to land a spot with the new Rocky Mountain K-9 Unit. They were still in their first year, on contract with the FBI to assist with cases across the region. The team was already on probationary status to determine its need, and thanks to a dangerous incident at the K-9 training center in Denver two months ago, they were under even more scrutiny. The case was still under investigation.

Regardless, Chris felt certain that tracking down and arresting Frank Lanier would help silence any fears about their team's future.

His boss, Tyson Wilkes, had created the concept of their Rocky Mountain K-9 Unit, recruiting officers he considered the best of the best. Their role was to interface with other law enforcement agencies to cover the wide expanse of the Rocky Mountains. Chris had been proud to be included, even though his relationship with his half brother, Ben Sawyer, also a RMK9 officer, was rocky. Ben was the one who'd recommended him to the sergeant in the first place.

Chris and Ben were professional at work, but their personal relationship was strained. Mostly because Ben kept trying to convince Chris to let go of his anger long enough to speak with their father. The father who'd had an affair with Chris's mother, but then dumped her because she wasn't part of the rancher community. Drew Sawyer had then married Ben's mother because she was not only from the community but came from the prosperous neighboring ranch, adding to his father's wealth.

Yeah, meeting the old man wasn't high on his list of things to do.

Not that it mattered now. He and Teddy had a killer to catch.

"I don't live far, and I have my Jeep." Lexie finally

stepped closer. "I'm sure I'll be okay getting the rest of the way home while you and Teddy go to work."

"Come a little closer." He dropped to a knee beside Teddy. "Friend, Teddy. Lexie is a friend." He held out his hand to Lexie. "Let him sniff you."

She looked interested as she placed her slender pale hand in his. A shock of awareness rippled up his arm, and he tried to mask the sensation by focusing on his partner.

Teddy sniffed for several long seconds, then his tail wagged back and forth with exuberance. Teddy was friendly by nature, unless threatened. He was also a phenomenal tracker, his nose one of the best of all K-9s on the team, second only to Nell the beagle.

At least in Chris's humble opinion. Besides, Nell was a cadaver dog. She didn't have Teddy's ability to find Lanier, who was alive and on the move.

"He's beautiful," Lexie murmured.

"Thanks. I think so, too." He rose to his feet, hiding a wince as his head began to pound again. "Ready?"

Lexie nodded. Before they moved, he took the evidence bag out of his pocket and offered Lanier's scent to Teddy. "This is Frank. Seek Frank," he commanded. "Seek."

Teddy sniffed and then lowered his nose, following the scent all the way outside.

Chris scanned the area outside the hangar, holding Teddy at bay as Lexie shut down the lights and locked the door. He noticed a dark blue Jeep parked off to the side from the main entrance.

"Seek," he repeated. Lexie watched in apparent fascination as Teddy followed the scent across the parking lot toward a spot along the edge of the woods. Teddy alerted and sat.

Not surprising to learn Lanier had sought cover in the forest. "Good boy. Heel, Teddy."

The dog looked back at him, as if he wanted to keep going, but then spun around and returned to his side. Chris quickly returned to Lexie and escorted her to the Jeep.

"He's amazing," she said in awe. "I've never seen a K-9 in action before."

"He is," Chris agreed. Teddy's nose kept working, as he sniffed around the vehicle. Thankfully, Teddy didn't alert at the Jeep, so he felt certain Lanier was hiding in the woods.

Lexie unlocked the car and opened the door. He tightened his grip on her arm and looked in the back seat and the rear storage area before nodding and releasing her. "It's clear."

"Thanks." Her smile was tremulous. "Take care of yourself, Officer."

"Chris." He wasn't sure why he corrected her. After all, he was a cop. "You, too, Lexie." He thrust a business card into her hand. "Here's my contact information. Don't hesitate to call if you need something."

She nodded, tucked the card away and slid behind the wheel. He waited until she was safely locked inside the vehicle before offering Teddy Lanier's scent once again.

"Seek," he commanded.

Teddy was eager to get back to work. His partner picked up Lanier's scent and trotted quickly toward the trees lining the far side of the parking lot. Chris pulled his weapon, something he should have done when he'd approached the hangar. When he'd first heard muffled voices, he hadn't anticipated Lanier had gone inside and taken a hostage.

A failure he'd have to own. He inwardly winced at

how Tyson would take the news. Then he shook it off. He still had a good chance of bringing Lanier into custody.

"Seek," he encouraged his partner as the dog wound his way around trees and brush. Chris held his flashlight nestled between two fingers of his left hand, using that same hand to help stabilize the gun he was holding with his right.

Sweeping his light over the area, he hoped to catch a glimpse of Lanier. It was risky to go after him in the woods, as Tyson Wilkes had told them at an earlier team meeting that Frank Lanier was known to be armed and dangerous. Something he now knew from firsthand experience.

But Chris didn't have a choice. The cold-blooded killer had already tried to kidnap a pilot. Who knew what else Lanier would do if he was feeling desperate.

It was Chris's job, and Teddy's, to keep the heat on. The longer Lanier was on the run, the more likely he'd make a mistake.

Teddy backtracked twice, but then remained hot on Lanier's trail. Chris's head pounded more at the fast pace, but he refused to succumb to pain or weakness. Once he might have prayed to God for strength, but not anymore.

Not after learning his mother had lied to him about the identity of his father. Something he'd only discovered after her death. And when Ben, his half brother, had reached out to him, to let him know their dad wanted to talk.

Whatever. The team was his life now. Sergeant Tyson Wilkes had recruited officers from all across the Rocky Mountain region. Tyson had served as an army ranger in Afghanistan, and had arranged for his Dutch shepherd mix, Echo, to return home with him. Ben was also a former army ranger and worked with his Doberman, Shadow. The other team members were Nelson Rivers and his K-9, Diesel, Danielle Vargas and Zana, Reece Campbell and Maverick, Harlow Zane and Nell, and Lucas Hudson and Angel.

Chris liked the way the team felt a bit like a family. As an only child, or so he'd thought, he'd always wanted brothers and sisters.

Now he had Ben and a slew of others. His personal relationship with Ben was something he needed to come to grips with sooner rather than later.

When his K-9 partner alerted near a fallen tree, Chris gratefully paused to take a breath. Teddy sat and looked up at him, expecting his reward.

"Good boy," he praised, rubbing the spaniel's silky brown-and-white fur. He pulled the spaniel's favorite toy, a small stuffed bear, from the backpack and offered it as a reward. Chris figured Lanier must have stopped here to rest. The guy had been on the run for well over fourteen hours after escaping from the transport van that was found at the side of the road just outside Helena. Lanier had been the only prisoner inside, as he was being taken to Helena for a sentencing hearing after being convicted of killing a banker. It still wasn't clear how Lanier had managed to escape. All they knew for sure was that the deputy had been found in the front seat of the van, shot in the head, presumably with his own gun. There was no sign of Lanier in or around the badly damaged van.

As the van wasn't drivable, they suspected Lanier to have stolen a vehicle or to be on foot. When a witness called in a report of seeing the suspect in Great Falls, their suspicions of his having a vehicle were confirmed. Great Falls was ninety miles from Helena.

Chris gently took the toy back, returned it to the pack, then pulled out the evidence bag. Inside was a scrap of fabric from Lanier's prison suit so that his K-9 could refresh the scent. "This is Frank. Seek Frank!"

Teddy lowered his nose to the ground, then lifted it into the air, drawing in the air around him, searching for the scent cone that would lead him to Lanier. Then Teddy bounded over the fallen log, picking up Lanier's scent on the other side.

Chris didn't keep Teddy on a leash, which was yet another risk. He valued Teddy's life more than his own, but leashes and woods didn't mesh well. And he needed to grip his gun and flashlight in two hands.

Chris quickened his pace to keep up, following his partner's lead. The dog headed northwest, the ground sloping downward beneath his feet.

"Good boy," he encouraged, as he continued scanning the area. He and Teddy were both wearing bullet-resistant vests, but their heads were not protected. Chris had no idea how good of a shot Lanier was, hoping the guy didn't have the skills to hit either of them from a distance, especially through the trees.

When Chris heard running water, his spirits sank. Teddy continued following Lanier's scent in a zigzag pattern.

But all too soon, Teddy came to a stop at the edge of the Sun River. It was a small river that branched off from the much larger Missouri River that snaked through town.

The dog alerted, then sat and gazed up at him, tongue lolling.

"Good boy, Teddy." Chris bent over to lavish praise

on the K-9, offering the toy bear again, even as the implication sank deep.

It galled him to admit Frank Lanier had used the river to mask his scent. The guy was smart, but Chris wasn't ready to give up so easily.

He let his partner rest a few minutes, then tried to estimate which way Lanier had taken. Likely west, since heading east would take them closer to town.

"Come. Seek." Chris walked along the riverbank. Teddy followed. He sniffed the ground, then lifted his nose into the air, as if trying to capture the elusive scent.

After about thirty yards, Chris picked Teddy up into his arms and crossed the river. On the other side, he went back toward the original spot where his partner had lost the scent, hoping his partner would pick it back up.

But there was nothing. According to Teddy's keen nose, there was no indication Lanier had gotten out of the river along this stretch.

Chris blew out a frustrated breath and sat down on a fallen log. Despite his and Teddy's best efforts, they'd lost him.

It was disheartening to accept the fact he needed to call his boss with the news that their escaped convict was still on the loose.

TWO

Lexie sat in her Jeep parked in front of her cabin for several long minutes, unable to shake off the events that had unraveled at the hangar. Not just the sweaty man who'd attacked her and tried to force her to fly him out of Great Falls, Montana—but the handsome K-9 cop who'd come to her rescue.

Secrets.

Logically, she knew Chris had meant he'd find Lanier's secrets. Not hers. But the image of the man in the photograph was still clear in her mind.

There was something about him. But what? Had to be that she caught a glimpse of him on the news. Lanier couldn't be connected with her past.

Her real name was Savannah Abigail Hall, and she was born twenty-eight years ago to Gerald and Abigail Hall. She'd grown up in New York with her parents and older brother, Jeremy. They hadn't wanted for anything, and honestly, if asked she would have said they had the perfect life. She'd even followed in her father's and uncle's footsteps working on Wall Street as a financial investor, which was ultimately how she'd learned her father's income had come from illegal means. All the money that had bought them the best house, nice cars, luxury vacations had come from her father's participation in everything from insider trading to Ponzi schemes. While her dad was partnered with his brother, she hadn't seen any evidence Uncle Ron was involved, too.

Horrified at her discovery, she'd confronted her father. Instead of being contrite, he'd bluntly told her to mind her own business, or else.

It was the *or else* that stayed with her. Because the look in her father's eyes when he'd threatened her had convinced her he'd do anything to keep his wealth. And his secrets.

Even if that meant silencing her, forever.

Shortly after her confrontation with her father, Lexie had discovered she was being followed. Then someone broke into her apartment. Realizing her father meant exactly what he'd said, she felt as if she had no choice but to disappear on her own.

Permanently.

The last five years hadn't been easy, but she'd survived. And eventually had thrived. She'd taken only her own hard-earned cash out of her personal bank account, twenty-five thousand dollars, to finance her future. Her finance skills had helped grow her savings until she could buy her own plane, rent the space at Blue Skye Aviation and the small cabin she called home.

But the near assault in the hangar brought her old fears rising back to the surface.

What if Chris was right about secrets never staying buried?

Lexie pulled out her phone and quickly searched her parents' social media pages. The pages started to

load, then froze, her parents' smiling faces looking ee-
rily back at her. She grimaced and put her phone away.
Internet access out here in the woods was hit or miss,
which was why she did most of her work at the hangar.
The radar system and storm-tracking software both
required high-speed internet access to work properly.

Drawing a deep breath, she climbed out of the
car. Her cabin was small, cozy and well off the main
highway. Perfect for her needs, and seeing it now, she
couldn't imagine her father would find her here. Not
after all this time, and not under her new name.

Not to mention, her new career as a pilot.

Lexie unlocked the door and cast a furtive glance
over her shoulder, before heading inside. It occurred to
her that having a dog like Teddy to alert her about im-
pending danger might be nice.

For the first time in what seemed like forever, Lexie
walked through her small cabin, checking each room,
under the bed, and finally the pantry and two closets, to
make sure no one was there. Paranoid? Maybe, but after
what she'd been through, she figured she was allowed.

Taking a seat at her desktop computer, she tried to
check on her parents again. This time, the page loaded,
showing her parents and her uncle dressed to the hilt at
a political fundraiser, accompanied by her older brother,
Jeremy, before the image froze. She hit the refresh key
several times, then shut it down.

She turned away, satisfied that her family was still
back in New York City, happily living their luxurious
lifestyle.

For a moment, she considered making another anonymous call to the Securities Exchange Commission. As
far as she could tell, nothing had happened after her

previous calls to the SEC to let them know of her father's illegal business dealings. The first call had been five years ago, followed by one every year thereafter.

Including one a few months ago.

Would another anonymous call matter? She had no way of knowing if the SEC had investigated her father's business practices, especially since her parents' image on social media made it appear like business as usual.

With a sigh, Lexie washed up and got ready for bed. Her tour flight was scheduled at ten the following morning. Plenty of time to return to the hangar to get an update on the weather conditions before heading out.

But sleep didn't come easily. She tossed and turned, unable to shut down the memories of her tumultuous past.

Of a father who would have killed her without a second thought to keep his illegal business ventures churning out money.

She finally fell into a light doze, only to be woken by a muffled noise. It wasn't as if living in the mountains was quiet; nocturnal animals roamed freely in the wilderness, hunting food. Hearing the screech of a bobcat or the growl of a wolf wasn't unusual.

Lexie strained to listen but heard nothing but silence. She slid out of bed, and eased toward her bedroom window, peering through the narrow crack between the curtains.

She didn't see anyone or anything. Then again, she hadn't seen anything earlier at the hangar until it was too late. The memory made her shiver.

The wind picked up a bit compared with earlier. Leafy branches swayed back and forth with vigor. Was that what she'd heard? Remembering how Chris and

Teddy had headed out to track Lanier made her fear seem foolish. The pair had likely found Frank Lanier by now.

She needed to let it go.

Peering at her watch, she realized it was four in the morning. Going back to sleep would be useless, especially now that adrenaline was pumping through her bloodstream. She headed into the kitchen and proceeded to make a pot of coffee. Considering her lack of sleep, and her upcoming tour, she figured she'd need every drop.

After two cups of coffee and breakfast, Lexie felt better. She needed to stop letting her imagination run wild. Five years had passed since Savannah Abigail Hall had dropped off the face of the earth. Tour pilot Lexie McDaniels didn't have anything to worry about.

She arrived at the hangar by eight o'clock. She was surprised that mechanic Skip Taylor wasn't there yet. Skip was in his late fifties and loved planes more than people. The cantankerous man spent his time tinkering with the plane engines, taking pride in keeping them in top-notch condition.

Refusing to think about the events of the previous night, Lexie went to her office and booted up the computer. As the satellite images and the storm-tracking software bloomed on the screen, she was relieved to see the forecast of clear skies for the upcoming day hadn't changed. The wind had calmed down, too, so she didn't foresee any problems from that end.

Hopefully, the tourists didn't suffer from motion sickness. People often assumed that because they had no trouble flying in commercial jets, they'd be fine.

Smaller planes like hers offered a very different and,

in her humble opinion, better experience. She could fly at lower altitudes, providing tourists with breathtaking views that couldn't be seen from the seat of a commercial plane.

The phone rang. The local cop on the other end of the line asked for information on the assault. She assumed Chris had reported the incident and verified what had taken place. The officer seemed satisfied with her account of the events. He promised to call back if he learned anything more.

Since she had time to kill, Lexie continued searching for information on her father. The photos from the political fundraiser were still on social media and had been taken just two days ago. When she heard the hangar door being unlocked and rolled open, she minimized her screen and strode over.

"Skip? Is that you?"

"Yeah, why? Who were you expecting?" Skip's sarcasm made her smile.

"No one, just making sure." She debated whether to let the older man know about the attack. While it was doubtful Lanier would come back here, Skip was thin and wiry, and combined with his age of fifty-eight, vulnerable. She'd feel terrible if something happened to him. She crossed over to meet up with him.

"Skip, there was an incident here last night. Did you hear on the news about that escaped convict? His name is Frank Lanier. He showed up here last night and tried to force me to fly him out of here."

"What? Are you okay?" Skip's sharp gaze raked over her. "How did you get away from him?"

"Thankfully, I'm fine. A police officer and his K-9 partner tracked Lanier here, arriving just in time to rescue me. I'm hoping they caught him by now, but if not, you need to avoid staying here alone late at night."

"Me? What about you?" Skip planted his hands on his narrow hips. "Sounds like you're the one in danger."

She forced a smile. "Probably, but be careful, anyway, okay?"

"Yeah, yeah," he groused.

"Would you mind handling the checklist on my plane, first?" she asked, changing the subject. "I have a tour heading out at ten."

"That's my job, ain't it?" Skip seemed more cranky than usual, but she let it go.

"Lexie?" The sound of her name had her spinning around to the door. Her eyes widened in surprise when she saw Chris and Teddy standing in the opening.

"Chris, I was just letting our mechanic, Skip Taylor, know about Frank Lanier coming here last night." She searched his keen topaz gaze. "Did you and Teddy find him?"

"No, unfortunately he escaped." Chris's expression turned grim. "I wanted you to know he's still on the loose, so that you'd make sure to take necessary precautions."

She swallowed hard. "Funny, I was just telling Skip the same thing."

"Everyone in Great Falls should be on the lookout for this guy." Chris took several steps into the hangar, the spaniel sniffing with interest. "But especially here, since Lanier may still try to force the issue of flying out of the area."

Her stomach tightened at the possibility, but she managed a nod. "Thanks for the warning."

"I got work to do," Skip mumbled, turning away to seek refuge with his planes.

Lexie wondered if she should cancel her tour or move on with life as usual.

"I want you to know, we'll continue searching for him," Chris said, breaking into her thoughts. "Chances are good that Lanier is long gone. But until we find him…" His voice trailed off.

"I spoke to the police about the attack last night." She frowned. "I only have one tour scheduled today. The family of four should be here in less than an hour. Do you think I need to cancel?"

Chris considered this, then shook his head. "No, I hate to make you do that. In fact, it would help if you'd look around while you're flying overhead, see if you can find any indication Lanier is still around."

"I can do that," she agreed.

"I think it would be good if Teddy and I hang out here until you return."

She was surprised by his offer. "That would be great, thanks."

"I'm going to take Teddy around, have him check things out." Chris waved a hand. "Don't worry about me. Just do what you need to do."

"Thanks again." She tucked her hands into the pockets of her jeans, watching as the handsome cop led his K-9 around the building.

Lexie tried to understand why she was drawn to Chris Fuller. It wasn't just his outward appearance, attractive as it was. No, there was something else.

She'd caught a hint of pain shadowing his gaze, only for an instant. As if someone close had hurt him.

A similar feeling was mirrored in her heart.

* * *

Chris had offered to stay to keep an eye on Lexie and the hangar but knew he should keep tracking Frank Lanier. The sooner he and Teddy found this guy, the better.

He'd only taken time off to rest his K-9 partner. Scent dogs needed to rest often, and to be kept hydrated. At dawn, they'd returned to the spot on the Sun River where they'd lost Lanier's scent, but had been unable to pick it up again.

Because the cold-blooded killer was gone? The guy could have easily made his way into town, using a stolen vehicle or hijacking another one to escape.

It was easier than thinking of the possibility Lanier was hiding nearby, biding his time until he could make another attempt to catch a plane ride out of the area.

Leaving Montana for good.

Chris watched Teddy carefully, but so far the only alerts his K-9 partner provided were in the main area where he and Lanier had physically struggled. In fact, there was still a smear of his blood on the concrete floor.

A sobering reminder that Lanier had gotten the best of him.

Next time, Chris silently promised. Next time, he would not let the convict escape.

After leaving Lexie last night, he'd reported the incident to the local police. He was glad to hear the officer had followed up with her by phone. When Lexie's tour group showed up, he kept Teddy off to the side and out of the way. The parents were nicely dressed, the teenage kids looking bored, until Skip pulled the plane out toward the hangar door.

"Cool, can I fly it?" The teenage boy eyed the plane with anticipation.

"I'm afraid not, liability rules." Lexie's words sounded canned, as if she was forced to say them often.

And she probably was.

After a few minutes, Lexie opened the door and helped her tourists up and into the plane. Then she went around and climbed into the cockpit. He wondered if he should have asked to ride along, but the plane wasn't that large, and he wasn't about to leave Teddy behind.

Once Lexie had taken the plane airborne, he turned his attention to the hangar. Skip had mostly ignored him and Teddy, clearly preferring working on engines to chatting with people.

His phone rang. Pulling it from his backpack, he winced when he saw Tyson's number. He'd left a message for his boss last night but hadn't heard back.

"Fuller," he answered.

"I got your message. I'm sorry to hear Lanier is still on the loose."

"It's my fault." Chris quickly took ownership for the loss. "I shouldn't have let him get the drop on me."

"Sounds like you did your best, considering Lanier had taken a woman hostage," Tyson said calmly. "I'm confident you and Teddy will find him."

Chris wasn't sure he deserved his boss letting him off the hook so easily. "The guy is smart. We lost his scent in the river. Have there been any other reported sightings? Or reports of stolen vehicles?"

"Nothing yet," Tyson responded.

Chris blew out a breath. If Lanier had stolen or hijacked a car, they should have heard about it by now. "Okay, any news on the missing woman?" Valentina

Silva, a twenty-five-year-old tourist, had recently disappeared and was feared abducted. She was last seen in
the Wellsville Mountains in Utah. Unfortunately, Valentina was one of several missing women in the region.
Each of the victims was tall, blue-eyed and blonde. The
FBI had asked the RMKU for help searching the expan-
sive area for any sign of the missing women.

As if having an escaped convict out there wasn't bad
enough, there was also a possible serial killer lurking
nearby.

"No." Tyson's tone turned somber. "I really hope she
doesn't turn up dead like the first two."

"Me, too." Normally, he'd pray for the missing
women, and Lexie, too. But his relationship with God
was rocky at the moment, so he thrust the urge aside.
"What about the missing baby?"

Chris hoped the infant, Chloe Baker, would be found
soon. Two months ago, one of their officers had responded to a car on fire in Denver, finding the female
driver unconscious nearby—along with an empty car
seat and baby blanket. That woman, Kate Montgomery,
was still in a coma. Not long after she'd been found,
police had discovered a deceased woman in a car in a
gulley, and she'd been identified as Nikki Baker—the
missing baby's mother. The team was working around
the clock to investigate the case but so far, there were
few answers. What had happened to the baby? What
was the connection between the women?

"We searched Baker's apartment. It's modest, exactly what you'd expect from a part-time, work-from-
home bookkeeper."

Chris frowned. "Except for the gold Rolex that was
found, right? That doesn't fit, does it?"

"You're right about that. But the initials, S.M., engraved inside aren't Ms. Baker's. We're working on connecting those initials to someone in her life, but nothing yet." Tyson sighed. "Kate Montgomery, who'd been found near the car fire, remains in the hospital in a coma. Her vitals are stable, but she still hasn't woken up. We desperately need to talk to her to find out more about the missing baby and who might have taken her."

Chris tried to inject confidence into his tone. "Our team is made up of the best. We'll figure it all out, you'll see. And I'll find Lanier, too. Teddy and I went back to the river once already, but I think I'll take him farther, see if we can pick up Lanier's scent."

"Sounds like a plan." Tyson hesitated, then said, "He could be out of the Great Falls area by now."

"I know. But until we have any other sightings of the guy, I may as well stay close to his last known whereabouts."

"Keep me posted, Chris."

"Will do." He was about to put his phone away when it rang again. He lifted a brow, as the caller was his half brother. "Hey, Ben."

"How's the tracking going?" Ben asked.

"Not as well as I'd like," he was forced to admit. "Unfortunately, we lost Lanier's trail in the river."

"I'm confident you and Teddy will find your quarry," Ben assured him. "You make a good team."

He appreciated Ben's ongoing support. It was more than he deserved. "How are Jamie and the baby?" Ben had fallen in love with the pregnant witness he'd been assigned to protect in Denver before a trial. Barbara June had been born prematurely. Ben had been there throughout Jamie's labor and delivery. Jamie had named the baby after Ben's mother. "They're good, both healthy and strong, but that's not why I called. I wanted you know our dad went in for another doctor's appointment this morning. They've scheduled him for a stress test next week to check out his heart. Depending on what they find, they may have to do a cardiac catheterization."

Chris blew out a breath at this news. Ben had been encouraging him to reach out to their father, something he'd stubbornly resisted. "I'm sorry to hear this."

"Yeah, me, too." Ben was silent for a moment, then said, "You really need to visit him, Chris. He wants to be a part of your life."

Grappling with a surge of emotion, he stared out at the wooded area surrounding the hangar. "I'm in the middle of a case, Ben. I can't leave Montana, unless it's to follow Lanier."

"You could have visited with him before this case came up," his brother pointed out. "But that doesn't matter. I don't expect you to go now, but soon, Chris. You really need to see him, before it's too late."

"Okay, I'll do my best." He didn't want Ben to argue further, so he quickly added, "Thanks for the update. I truly hope his stress test goes well."

"Please, Chris." Ben's low voice hit hard. "Do this for him. And for me."

"I will." The words popped out of his mouth before he could yank them back. "Talk to you later, Ben." Chris disconnected from the line before his brother could say anything more.

Heart problems. Stress test. He grimaced and glanced at Teddy. "I guess we'll be taking a trip to the Double S ranch in Wyoming when this case is over."

The idea of visiting his father filled him with dread. Chris knew he should be over it already. He hadn't learned about his mother's lies until after she died. It had been a shock to discover the long letter she'd hidden in her safe-deposit box. One in which she explained how she'd never married his father because he'd ended their affair, bowing under his family's pressure to marry someone of their same status and background, to increase the value of the ranch that was suffering a bit of a financial crisis. Enter Barbara, who fit the bill perfectly.

Even more surprising was that his father was still alive, not dead as he'd been told.

He hated knowing that his father had lived on his vast cattle ranch while he and his mother had struggled to make ends meet.

Yet he also knew his mother's lies had created the situation. She could have easily told Drew she was pregnant and asked for child support payments.

Only she hadn't. Because she was too proud? He had no way of knowing what had gone through her mind. Besides, it was too late to go back and change the past.

Somehow, he'd have to find a way to let go of his anger and resentment long enough to make good on his promise.

THREE

Lexie gently banked the plane into a wide curve, providing her tourists a breath-taking view of the Rocky Mountains. This was the final loop before she'd head back to the landing strip that would return them to the hangar.

Thankfully, her guests hadn't gotten air sick, and even the bored teenagers had perked up at the incredible sight below. It made her smile when she heard their exclamations. God's hand had been at work here, as He'd created the snowcapped Rocky Mountains, the rivers and streams. Flying high in the sky, seeing the beauty stretched out below, never failed to provide a sense of peace.

This was so much better than working on Wall Street.

As she'd flown over the area, Lexie had kept a keen eye out for anything unusual, but she didn't see anyone who looked out of place among the townsfolk of Great Falls.

Spotting someone on the ground from this altitude wasn't easy, but that didn't stop her from trying. She was deeply concerned about Lanier being on the loose.

What if he made another attempt to force her to fly

him out of Montana? Taking her own advice and sticking close to others may not be enough of a deterrent.
The owner of Blue Skye Aviation was Harry Olson.
He was five years older than Skip, and in her personal
opinion, neither man was in the best shape. Not over-
weight, but not exuding massive physical strength. Especially against an armed and dangerous man who'd
already killed a deputy while trying to escape, and
likely wouldn't hesitate to do so again.

She'd felt safe with Chris and Teddy, but the K-9 cop
and his partner would head out to continue searching
for Lanier the moment she returned to the hangar.

Hopefully, Lanier was long gone. She didn't want
to cancel her tours. Summer provided her best income
stream, helping to hold her over during the long, snowy
winters.

As she approached the runway, she caught a glimpse
of a man and dog walking toward the hangar. Seeing the
K-9 cop and his springer spaniel made her smile. One
of the teenagers gasped a bit as she landed the plane.
There was always a slight bounce when landing a plane,
even with the most experienced pilot.

As she taxied toward the hangar, she overheard her
guests gushing about how much they enjoyed the flight.
It was on the tip of her tongue to tell them to spread the
word about her flight tours, but she managed to refrain.

Her brochures were at every local restaurant and
hotel in Great Falls, as well as online. Word-of-mouth
advertising was important, but better left natural, rather
than forced.

Lexie removed her headset and turned to grin at her
passengers. "We're all set. Thanks so much for coming."

"Can we do this again, Dad?" one of the teens asked.

"Only if you want to pay the fee," the older man shot back. "Besides, it's time to head back to town for lunch. We have that hike this afternoon, remember?"

The teens looked at each other, shrugged and jumped down from the plane. Their parents followed and soon Lexie was shaking hands and bidding the foursome farewell.

Chris and Teddy came into the hangar, watching with interest as she and Skip moved the plane inside. The craft was light enough that it was easily done with two people.

"How was the flight?" Chris asked.

"Better than most." She grinned. "No puking is always a good thing."

Chris grimaced. "Does that happen often?"

"More than I'd like." She waved a hand. "It's no big deal, part of the job."

"Good attitude," he said wryly. "Are you ready to go?"

She glanced around the hangar. Harry had two planes. One was a Cessna like hers, the other a Beechcraft. Harry didn't have any tours scheduled for the next couple of days as he was visiting his daughter and new grandson in Billings. No reason to hang around, not if Lanier was still out there, hiding in the woods. "Yeah, sure. Give me a few minutes to finish some paperwork. We need to make sure Skip leaves for the day, too."

"Bah, I'm not going anywhere," the mechanic grumbled. "Need to work on Harry's plane. The Cessna needs a new fuel pump."

Lexie arched a brow at Chris, silently asking the officer to convince Skip to leave when they did. He gave a brief nod, indicating he'd do his best. Lexie turned and hurried into her cubicle-like office. She made a few notes on the flight plan she'd used for her tour, then filed it. Always good to have documentation in case customers came back for either a new tour or to file some sort of complaint.

The latter didn't happen often, thankfully, but she followed her usual routine, regardless. Hearing voices as Chris spoke to Skip, she decided to do another quick search on her father.

Typing "Gerald Hall" into the search engine, she waited for the latest news to pop up on the screen. The most recent photo, taken just yesterday, showed her father and her uncle Ron shaking hands with a New York City mayoral candidate.

It seemed her father was too busy furthering his business ventures to worry about her. Which was a good thing.

She stared at the photo for a moment. When she heard Chris's footsteps, she quickly minimized the screen and rose, standing purposefully in front of the monitor. "So, what's the verdict?"

"He's stubborn, but finally agreed to leave." Chris hesitated, then added, "Teddy alerted on a boot print from Lanier out in the woods, about fifty yards from here. Sharing that information with Skip helped change his mind. He decided the fuel pump could wait."

Her stomach sank at the news of finding a boot print, but she did her best not to show her fear. "That print could have been left at any point prior to the attack. There wasn't any rain last night."

"Could be," Chris agreed. "We're still going to check out the entire area again this afternoon, just to be sure."

She couldn't help glancing apprehensively through

the open hangar door to the woods beyond. "You really think he stayed hidden in the woods nearby?"

"I can't afford to assume anything one way or the other," Chris said evenly. "It's my job to follow the facts. But don't worry, if Lanier is still out there, Teddy will find him."

After seeing the K-9 in action, she didn't doubt the spaniel's skills. She headed out of the hangar, then waited for Skip to follow, before closing and locking the large overhead door. She found herself wishing Harry had installed security cameras around the building. They hadn't been needed before now. Great Falls wasn't a high-crime area; normally she felt very safe here.

But not so much with Lanier on the loose.

Chris walked Teddy around her Jeep, commanding the dog to seek. When he was satisfied, he gestured toward it. "It's safe. I'll follow you to your place."

"Okay." It was a little unnerving to have her own personal police escort, but she slid behind the wheel. Chris opened the back of his SUV so Teddy could jump inside, then put his pack in the back seat. Lexie waited for Skip to leave the parking lot first, before following him. Skip's place was located in the opposite direction, so they quickly parted ways, Skip heading south, while she went north.

Chris's SUV stayed behind her the entire way, including all the way up her curvy and rugged driveway to the cabin. Using the button on her visor, she opened the garage door and drove inside. When she pushed her driver's door open, Chris waved her back.

"Stay inside, Lexie. Wait until Teddy and I clear the place."

She nodded, returned to her seat and closed the car door. Chris didn't waste a moment in letting Teddy out and going to work.

"Seek," he commanded, taking the spaniel up toward the cabin. The dog sniffed eagerly, and she wondered how long it had taken Chris to train the animal. Being in the garage made it difficult to watch them for long, but even to her inexpert eye, dog and man were very much in tune with each other.

After a good fifteen minutes, the tall, handsome cop approached her Jeep. He surprised her by opening her door for her.

"All clear," he assured her. "Thanks for letting us check the place out."

"Of course. It's a relief to know Lanier hasn't been here." She pulled her house keys from her purse. "Thanks for the escort home. I don't suppose you can keep me updated on whether or not you find him? I have another tour scheduled tomorrow."

"I can do that. What's your phone number?"

She gave him the number and he quickly entered it into his phone. Giving him her personal information felt awkward, maybe because she secretly found him incredibly attractive. She strove for a professional tone. "Thanks."

"It's the least I can do. We'll do our best to find this guy." His expression turned thoughtful. "You mentioned another tour. What time tomorrow?"

"Same as today, ten in the morning. But I also have a tour tomorrow afternoon at one thirty as well." She winced as she realized her lapse. "There was something in the forecast about the threat of pop-up storms and I forgot to check the satellite before I left. My home computer internet isn't strong enough to load the software."

"Isn't it better to do that in the morning?" He frowned, resting his hand lightly on Teddy's brown-and-white head. The dog was incredibly well behaved. No, *well trained*, she inwardly corrected. Other than during the attack last night, she hadn't heard him growl or bark.

Lexie glanced up at Chris. "I generally do both, because weather patterns change quickly around here, especially the wind." She threaded her fingers through her hair, annoyed with herself for being distracted by thoughts of her father. "I'll just have to wait until morning."

As they left the garage, Chris glanced up at the puffy clouds dotting the sky, while following her up to the front door. After unlocking it, she stood in the threshold. "Looks fine for now," he said. "But if it's that important, I can escort you back to the hangar later."

His offer was touching. "Really? That would be great, although I'll pray that God will give you and Teddy the strength and wisdom to find Lanier very soon, so that it won't be necessary."

A pained expression darkened his amber eyes for a moment, but then it vanished. "That's the plan. Come, Teddy."

As Lexie closed the door and locked the door, she found herself wondering about Officer Chris Fuller. He was a good man, dedicated to the task of finding Frank Lanier. There was much to admire about him. Yet she couldn't help feeling a bit depressed that Chris didn't seem to be a believer.

Well, maybe not, but that wouldn't stop her from praying for him.

* * *

Lexie's offer to pray for him echoed through his mind as Chris headed back to the hangar. His mother, Vi, would be horrified to know he'd turned away from the church.

Then again, his mother had lied to him about his father. And wasn't that one of God's Ten Commandments? *Thou shalt not bear false witness.*

Whatever. Chris tried to shake off the mess of his personal life. Finding Lanier remained his sole priority. A mission he had no intention of failing.

He parked his SUV near the hangar, grabbed his backpack and let Teddy out. He made sure his partner was well hydrated before getting back to work.

After debating for a moment, Chris headed back to the spot along the Sun River where Teddy had lost Lanier's scent. He believed the escaped convict had used the water to mask his scent, a trick that had unfortunately worked.

But the guy had to have gotten out of the water at some point. He and Teddy just needed to find that spot.

Easier to do in the daylight, than at night, that was for sure.

The hike to the river didn't take long. Teddy alerted in the same area as the night before. This time, Chris walked much farther along the side of the riverbank, covering more ground than they'd been able to earlier that morning and the night before.

The terrain was rough in patches, and despite the mild temperatures, sweat rolled freely down his back, dampening his shirt. He and Teddy had grown accustomed to being in the mountains, it was far different than working the streets of Phoenix.

Things had changed so much in the past few months that he felt as if he were riding a roller coaster wearing a blindfold, each curve sharper than the one before.

Making it impossible to know what was coming up next.

He shook off the tumultuous thoughts. Sweeping his gaze over the area, he tripped over a tree root and nearly fell flat on his face. Somehow, he managed to catch himself, Teddy instantly coming to his side. He took a moment to give the spaniel some well-deserved attention. "I'm okay, boy. Let's keep going. Seek!"

Teddy wheeled around and went back to work. Chris raked his gaze over the area, knowing he needed to stay sharp.

They took frequent rest breaks, for Teddy's sake. When they'd gone almost three miles according to his smart watch, Teddy alerted.

"Good boy!" He praised the K-9, offering him his favorite bear, before crouching down to survey the area. A surge of satisfaction hit when he found a boot print. Chris took a moment to take a picture with his phone. He needed to get this to their K-9 team's forensic technical specialist, Russ Tate. He'd be able to find out if this brand of shoe could be narrowed down to a specific store, which might help in their search for Lanier. The boot print was their first tangible lead.

He called off the search to give Teddy a break, marking the location with a small flag, and memorized the coordinates via his GPS device, so he could find it again. Back at the motel, he sent the boot print to Russ, who promised to look into it.

Later that afternoon, he and Teddy returned to work. Upon reaching the area he'd flagged, they continued.

Dark clouds gathered overhead, and he belatedly remembered his promise to take Lexie back to the hangar. Soon, he told himself. There wasn't much daylight left, especially considering the storm clouds. She was right about how quickly the weather could change.

This time, Teddy followed a winding path, then alerted at the base of a large tree. The brush was flattened, as if Lanier had stretched out there to rest.

Chris offered Teddy some water from his canteen, before taking a sip for himself. This area wasn't nearly as dense. Checking his GPS tracker, he realized he was only a mile or so from Lexie's place.

His blood chilled at the realization, but he and Teddy had already searched the area around the cabin without finding any sign of Lanier being there. Putting his fear aside, he bent down to pet his K-9.

"You doing okay, Teddy?"

The spaniel wagged his tail and licked him.

"Seek!" As soon as Chris gave the command, Teddy wheeled around and quickly picked up Lanier's scent.

Ignoring his fatigue from a sleepless night, Chris followed in Teddy's wake. His partner soon alerted again, and this time, Chris found another boot print. A full boot print. Excited, he used his own foot as a measurement, and took several pictures with his phone. He'd send this to Russ, too, when they were finished.

Lexie was right about the internet access out here. His phone only had one bar, which wasn't ideal.

"Good boy," he praised Teddy. As he was about to give the command to keep going, his phone vibrated.

Chris pulled the device from his pocket, fully expecting to see his boss's number on the screen. Or his half brother's.

But it was Lexie's.

"Hello? Lexie?"

He heard choppy breathing on the other end of the phone, then nothing.

A chill snaked down his spine. Had the phone connection gone out? Or something more sinister?

He called her back, but his attempt went straight to voice mail.

The icy chill sank deep into his bones. Every one of his instincts screamed at him that something was wrong. Very, very wrong. Was it possible Lanier had gone to her cabin after all? That he'd waited deep in the woods for Chris and Teddy to leave, before making his move?

But if so, why not wait until dark?

There wasn't time to worry about the convict's intentions. "Teddy, heel!"

The spaniel instantly came to his side, looking up at him expectantly. Using his compass, Chris estimated the approximate location of Lexie's cabin.

"Come, Teddy!" Chris pulled his gun and broke into a run.

FOUR

Hiding in the pantry off her kitchen, Lexie pushed herself into the corner, her heart thundering in her chest. She'd been doing laundry when she'd heard glass shattering. Realizing someone was breaking into her house, she grabbed a butcher knife, and her phone. She'd quickly called Chris, praying he was nearby.

But then, the sound of footsteps grew louder. Swallowing a cry, she had remained silent, quickly disconnecting from the call. She couldn't let whoever was inside her home find her.

Clutching the knife, Lexie waited, each second passing with excruciating slowness. She stared at the knife in her hand, wondering if she'd have the fortitude to use it.

Listening beyond her pounding heart, she tracked the sound of footfalls as the intruder made his way through her cabin. Then she abruptly caught a whiff of an awful smell. The familiar putrid scent of body odor mixed with cigarettes was enough to make her gag.

Lanier was in her house!

Lexie bit her lip hard to keep from crying out. She knew only too well that Lanier had a gun. She shivered, trying not to panic. The pantry door had a handle, but no lock. Who would have thought you'd need one? The door also had shutter-like slats on the front, just enough of an opening between them for her to see through. Plastered in the corner, however, she couldn't see details, and was afraid to move closer.

A dark shape passed by her line of sight. Her stomach knotted painfully. He was so close! Right on the other side of the door. She held her breath, tightening her grip on the knife while desperately hoping and praying he wouldn't find her.

Please keep me safe, Lord!

The movement on the other side of the door stopped. What had gotten Lanier's attention? She forced herself to breathe, gathering her strength. The knife was a poor match against a gun, but maybe if she could catch him off guard? Yes. That was her only option.

She could do this. She *had* to do this.

The dark shape moved in front of the door. Her palms damped with sweat as she saw the shadow stay motionless for what seemed like an eternity.

Then the door handle began to move.

Lexie lifted the knife, prepared to bring it down on whatever part of Lanier's body came through the door. She fully expected he'd lead with the gun.

Suddenly the handle stopped turning and the shadow moved away. She blinked, stared, wondering if she'd imagined the entire thing. But no, she could hear heavy footsteps moving away, no attempt at secrecy now.

He was leaving? Why? Then a dog barked and she knew Chris and Teddy were close by.

"Lexie!" Hearing Chris shout her name made her

close her eyes and thank God for sending him to her rescue.

She opened the pantry door and poked her head out, surveying the kitchen. No one was there, but the horrible odor remained.

Or maybe it only lingered in her imagination.

"Lexie?" Chris's voice sounded as if he was in one of the bedrooms. "Are you okay?"

"Fine," she croaked, her throat still tight with fear. She swallowed hard and set the butcher knife on the counter.

Chris burst into the kitchen, his eyes wild until he saw her standing there. Then he surprised her by rushing forward to sweep her into his arms.

"I was afraid I was too late, that he'd already gotten to you," he whispered against her hair.

"I'm okay," she managed, her voice stronger this time. She clung to his broad shoulders, pressing her face against his neck, relishing his embrace. Chris's strength seeped into her, and she felt reassured by his presence.

"I'm glad I got here in time," he murmured.

"Me, too." For a long moment she hugged him, wishing she could stay with him forever, then forced herself to pull away. "Thanks for saving my life, Chris."

He stared down at her, his topaz gaze searching hers as if he wanted to stay something more.

A cold nose touched her hand. She glanced down at Teddy, smiling into his deep brown eyes. "Hey, boy."

"It was Lanier who broke in, right?" Chris demanded.

"Yes." Her smile faded. "I heard the sound of breaking glass and knew someone was inside. I grabbed a knife and my phone. That's when I tried to call you. I was hiding in the pantry, though, and too afraid to talk. I saw his shadow move past the door. Then the door handle started to turn." Reliving those moments of terror wasn't easy. "Something caused him to back away. You and Teddy must have scared him off."

Chris blew out a breath. "I was about to kick in the front door when I heard something around back. But by the time I got there, Lanier was gone." He grimaced. "Will you be okay here while Teddy and I try to find him?"

She swallowed a protest and nodded. "Yes, of course. Go ahead." Thunder rumbled overhead and rain began to fall. "You'd better hurry, though."

Chris surprised her by giving her hand a quick squeeze. "Be safe. We won't be too long."

"I understand." She winced at the rain pounding on the roof of her cabin. "You're going to get drenched."

"Won't be the first time," Chris said wryly. "Come, Teddy."

They headed out the back door. Lexie watched as Chris offered Teddy the scent bag. The dog went to work, alerting near the broken window, then taking off through her property and into the woods.

Lexie glanced around her cabin, her sanctuary, wondering if she'd ever feel safe here again. Why did Lanier keep coming after her? Why not Harry, who was also a pilot? Didn't the older man make for an easier target?

It was possible Lanier didn't know about Harry and had latched onto her either because of her flyers distributed all around town, or simply because he'd watched her flying in and out of the hangar. Still, she found his persistence to get to her odd.

Determined to keep busy, she found some plywood

in the basement, along with a hammer and some nails. Rain was pouring in through the broken window, so she boarded it up from the outside. She doubted the plywood would keep human predators out, but it was the best she could manage.

Afterward, she changed into dry clothes and paced, waiting for Chris and Teddy to return. What if Lanier managed to get the jump on them? She trusted in Chris and Teddy's abilities yet couldn't help fearing something would happen to them.

Thirty minutes later, she heard someone at the door. Relieved to see Chris and Teddy, she quickly let them in. They were both drenched.

"I have towels for you," she said, handing him two large bath towels. "Unfortunately, I don't have dry clothes that will fit you."

"This is perfect, thanks," he assured her. She was impressed at how Chris tended to Teddy first, drying the dog from nose to tail, before using one of the towels on himself.

"I guess you couldn't find him." She tried not to sound too disappointed.

"No, sorry. A heavy rain along with the wind can hamper the dog's ability to track the scent cone. It's not impossible, but not as easy and I've already worked Teddy longer than I planned. He deserves to rest." He grimaced and set his backpack aside. "There's always tomorrow."

"Okay." She didn't want any harm to come to Teddy, or to Chris, either.

He draped the towel over his shoulders and looked at her. "Did you pack a bag?"

"Uh, no." She glanced back toward where the bedrooms were located.

"You need to do that, Lexie. You can't stay here." Chris's tone was gentle but firm. "Lanier knows where you live, and I'm afraid it's only a matter of time before he'll be back."

She shivered. Fear, not the chill from the summer rain. She should have anticipated this. Five years ago, she'd managed to escape New York, create a new identity for herself. Obviously, she was out of practice.

"Give me a few minutes." She hurried down the hall to her bedroom. The broken window was in the guest room, but she couldn't help peering out into the darkness to make sure no one was out there. Satisfied Lanier was also hiding out from the storm, she grabbed a small suitcase and began tossing clothes inside.

When she emerged from the bedroom, she found Chris and Teddy still standing by the door. Despite the towels, water still dripped from their clothes. "I'm ready."

"Great." He opened the door, picked up his pack and glanced around the front yard. "We'll need to take your Jeep to the hangar where I left my SUV. Is that okay with you?"

"Sure. You can drive if you'd like." She tossed him her keys, glad to be going away from here. The isolation she'd loved about the cabin when she'd bought it wasn't nearly as attractive now.

Not with Lanier on the loose.

Chris couldn't believe Lanier had been so bold as to break into Lexie's cabin. How had he found out where she lived? He didn't like the way Lanier seemed to have targeted Lexie on a personal level. If she hadn't called him… He couldn't bear to finish the thought.

From what she described, Lanier was seconds away from finding her in the pantry before he and Teddy had sent him on the run again. The thunderstorms and wind gusts had made searching for Lanier nearly impossible. Teddy was always eager to work, but Chris hadn't been willing to risk injuring his partner.

His dog came first, always.

Yet it was extremely frustrating to lose this guy again. He scowled as he considered his next moves. The torrential rain made it difficult to see, forcing him to drive slowly along the winding roads toward Blue Skye Aviation.

If Lanier wanted a way out of Great Falls, Montana, flying wasn't his only option. Why not steal another car? Or hike to another town? Granted, the cities and towns weren't close together out here, but easily accomplished considering the amount of time this guy was wasting by hanging around here.

The whole scenario didn't make a lot of sense.

When he reached the hangar, he drove in a circle around the entire parking lot before pulling up alongside his SUV. He glanced at Lexie. "Stay here. I need to check out the vehicle just to verify it hasn't been tampered with."

She paled. "Okay."

He took his time investigating the area around his SUV. At this point, he wasn't about to put anything past Lanier. He felt for any tracking devices, then went as far as to crawl beneath the car, using his flashlight app to make sure there wasn't an explosive device planted beneath.

Finally, he went back to the Jeep. "We can drive together in the SUV," he said to Lexie. "It's designed specifically for K-9s. Can we park your Jeep inside the hangar?"

She hesitated, then nodded. "I have my keys and I'm sure Harry won't mind."

Fifteen minutes later, they were on the road heading into Great Falls. "I'm staying at a motel just outside of the city proper, and I'll get you a room next to mine, okay?"

"For how long?" Lexie's brow puckered. "I can't just sit around in a motel, not when I'm running a business."

He winced. "I know this is an imposition, but your safety is important."

"I agree," she hastened to reassure him. "I'm just hoping I'll be able to keep my tours going."

"I'll do my best to make sure you can." The offer popped out of his mouth before he could stop it. Why was he doing this? His job was to find Lanier, not to help Lexie keep her tourist business running.

Becoming emotionally involved with her wasn't smart. In more ways than one. He wasn't looking to become involved in a relationship, especially not with a woman he barely knew. Even if he was interested, Lexie was involved in his case, which made her off-limits. And once she wasn't involved in his case, he still wasn't interested. He'd tried a long-distance relationship once before, with disastrous results.

He and Debra had dated for a year, visiting each other as often as possible. His job required him to do a lot of traveling, and he'd driven between Denver where he lived to Cheyenne, Wyoming, as often as he could. But when he'd shown up in Cheyenne a day earlier than expected, he'd found Debra with another guy. Yeah, his visit had been a surprise, all right.

Not the good kind.

First his mother's lies, then Debra's. Maybe there was something wrong with him that women felt the need to lie to him. He gave himself a mental shake. There was no point in wallowing in the past.

Stay focused, Fuller, he warned. *Lexie's life depends on you finding Lanier.*

"I appreciate your help," Lexie said, breaking into his thoughts. "I just wish I knew why he's targeted me. I'm not the only one with a plane—or a vehicle."

He glanced at her. "I have to admit, that part is bothering me, too."

"Lanier escaped from Helena, right?" Lexie asked.

"Yeah, and Great Falls is ninety miles from there. Based on the time of his escape from the deputy, and then being seen in Great Falls, I believe he must have gotten a ride from someone, since we haven't received any reports of a stolen or hijacked care in Helena around the time he escaped. I figure Lanier must still have a vehicle, because the hangar is pretty far out of town for him to be on foot."

She frowned. "I haven't seen a strange car around here, have you?"

"No," he admitted. "But he could have it stashed somewhere nearby." Although if that was the case, shouldn't Teddy have found it?

"For sure he didn't have a car when he broke into my house," Lexie said. "He must have come through the woods on foot."

"Yeah." He thought back. "And there was no sign of a car in the area Teddy and I were searching, either."

Had Lanier hitched a ride into town, then stolen a car? He wouldn't put anything past the escaped convict.

Not after the way he'd callously killed a deputy to escape.

"Maybe he has a place between the hangar and Great Falls," Lexie said thoughtfully. "Either a rental or some abandoned dwelling."

"Good thinking," he said with admiration. "That's a great lead I can check out."

"I'm glad to help." She smiled, and he was struck again by how beautiful she was. Lexie seemed to be everything Debra wasn't, yet he refused to let down his guard.

Lexie was a woman who needed his protection, nothing more.

By the time they got settled into adjoining rooms, it was nine thirty at night. "Are you hungry? They deliver sub sandwiches if you're interested," he offered.

"That would be great, thanks."

"What would you like?"

"Turkey on whole wheat, with lettuce, tomatoes and pickles."

"Pickles?" he teased, lifting a brow.

"I love them," she said unapologetically before ducking into her room.

He called in the order, then changed out of his wet clothes. He took care of Teddy, who promptly stretched out on the bed to snooze.

Chris knew he'd worked his dog long and hard today. He smiled at Teddy, who snored softly. The spaniel was the best partner he'd ever had.

While he waited for the subs, Chris searched the local properties between Great Falls and the Blue Skye hangar. He found three possibilities and flagged them as places to investigate the following day.

A knock at his door roused Teddy. Chris peered through the window, then opened the door. "Thanks," he said, taking the bag and handing over a generous tip.

After Chris closed the door, Teddy fell back to sleep. He lightly rapped on the connecting door, before poking his head in. "Lexie? I have our subs."

"Come in." She used the remote to shut off the television.

He set the bag on the small table and pulled out their respective sandwiches as she crossed over to join him.

"I'm famished," she admitted. "Didn't make time for lunch."

"I thought as much." He was about to unwrap his sub when he noticed Lexie had bowed her head to silently pray.

He did the same, waiting for her to finish. His mother had always prayed before meals. He couldn't help but wonder why she'd done that, while she'd withheld the truth about his father from him. Had she used that time to also pray for forgiveness?

"This looks great," Lexie said, before taking a big bite of her sandwich. "Thanks."

"You're welcome." Her simple gratitude made him smile. He needed to stop rehashing the past. He'd never know why his mother had lied, and at this point it didn't matter. He reached into the bag and pulled out two small packages of chips, handing one to her.

"Where's Teddy?"

He jerked his thumb over his shoulder. "Sleeping. He worked hard today and deserves to rest."

"He's incredible," Lexie agreed.

"Since you live in the area, I'd like to show you the three properties I found." He rose and tiptoed into his room to grab his computer. Teddy snored softly and didn't so much as flick his ear. Setting the computer on the table, he opened it up and turned it toward Lexie. "Tell me what you know."

She ate a few chips while examining the screen. "The place closest to mine is owned by an older couple, the Jerichos. They're very sweet." She looked at him. "I hope Lanier didn't do something to harm them."

"I hope not, too. The local cops are keeping an eye out for Lanier, too. What about the others?"

"I think this place might be either a vacation type of place or abandoned." She turned the screen and leaned over to show him. "I have never seen anyone around."

"Okay, that one goes to the top of the list." He was keenly aware of her lilac scent. "And the third place?"

She grimaced. "Unfortunately, I don't know anything about that one. I never paid attention when driving past on my way into town."

"Okay, thanks. That's very helpful." He closed the computer. "I'm sure if Lanier found an abandoned place, he'd use that first rather than drawing unwanted attention to himself."

"I pray you're right, Chris." Her expression was troubled. Then she jumped up and picked up her phone from the bedside table. She scrolled through her contacts, then held the phone to her ear. "Mrs. Jericho? This is Lexie McDaniels. How are you and Abe doing? I wanted to check in after that storm blew through."

There was a pause, then she smiled with relief and said, "I'm happy to hear you're doing well. Take care." She sighed with relief. "They're safe."

"I'm glad," he said. "They didn't lose power, did they?"

"No, they have a generator, the same way I do." Lexie smiled as she resumed her seat.

"Your first tour is at ten o'clock tomorrow, right?" he said when they'd finished eating.

"Yes, but I'll need to be in earlier, as I didn't get a chance to check it last night. The wind changes often around here." She grimaced. "The way it did today."

"Understood." The thought of her flying into a storm made his stomach churn.

Lexie gathered their sandwich wrappers and tossed them in the garbage. Then she knocked him for a loop by leaning down to kiss his cheek. "Thanks again, Chris."

He couldn't speak, so he simply nodded and escaped through the connecting doorway.

So far, he was failing miserably at his goal of keeping Lexie McDaniels at a distance.

FIVE

Lexie slept well, reassured by Chris and Teddy's presence nearby. In the bright light of the morning, though, she winced at how she'd kissed his cheek.

What had gotten into her? The two recent near-death experiences must have impacted her psyche more than she realized.

She couldn't afford to get close to Chris. It wasn't fair, since she was hiding her true identity. These past five years had been good to her. She loved the slower pace, running her own tour business. No reason to yearn for something more.

Something she couldn't have.

After a quick shower, she made herself coffee from the small pot in the room. When she heard the door open, she froze.

"Lexie? You awake?"

Chris's deep voice brought a wave of relief washing over her. Calling herself all kinds of an idiot, she cleared her throat. "Yes, I'm up."

He poked his head through the connecting door. "I had to take Teddy out, and plan to feed him now. When he's finished, I thought we'd grab some breakfast before driving to the hangar, if that's okay with you?"

Of course he'd taken care of his dog. She smiled and nodded. "Sounds good, thanks."

While she waited, she used her laptop to bring up the satellite app. The motel internet was better than what she had at the cabin, although software still took a moment to load. She watched the weather pattern, satisfied that the storm had moved on and the current clear weather would stick around long enough for her tours to remain on schedule.

Now, if Lanier would stay away from her and the hangar, she'd feel even better.

Lexie was just about to pull up information on her father when Chris lightly rapped on their connecting door. "Teddy is set. Are you ready to go?"

"Yes." She closed her computer and stood. Then frowned at her duffel bag. "I notice you have your backpack. Should I take my duffel?"

"No, leave it. My pack is full of supplies that I might need while tracking our suspect. I don't want you going back to your cabin until we have Lanier in custody."

"In custody?" she echoed. "What if he's left the area?"

Chris nodded. "If we receive an alert that he's been seen in another area, then you'll be fine to return home."

It struck her that if Lanier moved on, Chris and Teddy would follow him. All the more reason to keep her chaotic emotions under control. The handsome K-9 cop was just passing through.

"There's a decent restaurant right across the street," he said as she looped her small purse over her shoulder and joined him at the doorway. He had Teddy on a leash. The dog wagged his tail, greeting her with a lick.

"The Blue Ox." She ran her hand over Teddy's soft fur. "I've eaten there. It's great."

"I take it their breakfasts are hearty enough for Paul Bunyan?" he joked.

She laughed. "You got it."

The Blue Ox was busy, packed with summer tourists. As they walked in, she automatically checked the side display to make sure her brochures for tour flights were available. There were plenty left, but she made a mental note to return later to add more, just in case.

"We don't allow dogs in here," the hostess said, looking harried.

"He's a K-9 cop, and will sit at my feet the entire time," Chris said firmly.

The woman looked down at Teddy as if just noticing his vest for the first time. She hesitated, then caved. "Fine. But if he causes a ruckus he's out of here."

"He won't."

Once they were seated, and had placed their orders, she gratefully sipped her coffee. True to Chris's word, Teddy rested beneath the table at their feet. "I think we should stop and check out that abandoned property on our way to the hangar."

His topaz eyes were sharp. "I plan to do that later. Once you're safe on your tour."

"But I know right where the property is," she argued, annoyed with his dismissive tone.

"And I have a GPS tracker," he countered. When she opened her mouth, he held up a hand. "I'm not putting you in danger, understood?"

She eyed him over the rim of her mug. "I appreciate that, but I also trust you and Teddy to keep me safe."

Their food arrived, putting an end to the discussion. Lexie bowed her head and thanked God for the meal, for keeping her safe, and for Chris and Teddy. When she lifted her head, she found Chris gazing down at his folded hands, as if he might have joined her in prayer.

Wishful thinking? Maybe.

When they finished eating, Chris took the bill. "I can pay my way," she protested.

"I've got it." His tone was all business this morning, as if their brief embrace yesterday hadn't happened.

Fine by her, she reminded herself. The sooner Chris found and arrested Lanier, the better. She wanted her life to go back to normal.

They headed back outside to where he'd left his SUV. Chris opened the hatch and Teddy nimbly jumped inside.

Chris was uncharacteristically quiet as he headed out of the small town to where the Blue Skye Hangar was located. When they were close to the area where the abandoned property was located, she reached out to lightly touch his arm.

"Slow down, the driveway should be up ahead on my side," she said.

"We're not stopping," he protested, although she noticed he gently pressed on the brakes.

"Fine, but you still need to know where the driveway is." She kept her gaze on the side of the road closest to her. Last she remembered the driveway was badly overgrown. "There! Stop!"

The SUV came to an abrupt halt. "Where?" Chris peered through her window.

"See those tire tracks?" Lexie found it difficult to breathe. As much as she'd wanted to stop here, seeing evidence that the abandoned property had been accessed recently hit her in the face like a slap. "Someone is definitely using the place."

Lanier? Or someone who'd recently bought the place?

Chris didn't say anything for a long moment, before

he put the SUV in gear and continued driving. "I'll head back with Teddy to investigate, once you're in the air."

This time, she didn't argue. The thought of seeing Lanier was enough to make her palms sweat. The memory of how he'd choked her, dragging her resolutely toward the plane, flashed through her mind.

She swallowed hard and pressed a hand to her stomach. Waiting until she was up in the air with her tour sounded like a good idea.

Facing danger while flying was one thing. Confronting an armed and dangerous escaped convict was something far different.

They arrived at the hangar about forty minutes before her tour was scheduled. Skip was already inside, puttering around her plane.

"Why is your Jeep in here?" Skip asked with a scowl. "Does Harry know you're storing it inside the hangar?"

"Good morning to you, too, Skip." She smiled and headed toward her Jeep. "Taking this outside now."

"Hrmph," she heard before climbing in.

She was keenly aware of Chris and Teddy standing nearby as she went through her usual routine. Skip helped her pull her plane out so they could go through the checklist.

"She's fueled and ready to go," Skip finally announced.

"Great. I think my tour group just pulled in." The group comprised four women who were driving their way across the US. They were giggling and laughing as they emerged from the car.

She glanced at Chris, who watched them intently. The women posed no threat in her opinion, but she appreciated his remaining on high alert. There was no denying his protective attitude was attractive. She couldn't remember the last time any man had really cared about her safety.

Then again, she'd never been attacked by an escaped convict who'd murdered at least two people, either.

Lexie greeted her guests and helped them climb up into her plane. She jumped into the pilot's seat, placing the headphones over her ears.

As she taxied her plane toward the runway, she glanced back at Chris and Teddy. The duo was already heading back to Chris's SUV, no doubt anxious to investigate the abandoned property.

She sent up a silent prayer for their safety, even as she increased her speed and pulled on the stick to ease the plane up and off the ground.

Hopefully, by the time she'd returned, Chris and Teddy would have Frank Lanier in custody.

Yet deep down, she couldn't bring herself to truly believe it would be quite that easy.

Chris made sure his bullet resistant vest was secure, then bent over to adjust Teddy's. The recent tire tracks coming from the abandoned property made him think Lanier had stumbled across the place and was using it as his hideout.

He considered calling on the Great Falls police department for backup, then decided against it. The property wasn't that far out of town. If Teddy alerted to Lanier's scent, then he'd make the call.

Nothing would give him more satisfaction than to arrest Frank Lanier.

He parked on the road twenty feet from the end of the driveway and let Teddy out. He didn't put the K9 on leash, in case Lanier was hanging around and started shooting. It was important for the dog to have the freedom to run away.

Springer spaniels weren't known for being attack dogs, yet Chris knew that Teddy would not hesitate to protect him from any perceived threat. Which was why he couldn't afford to place his partner in that position.

He put Teddy to work, moving cautiously up the tire-rutted driveway, his senses on full alert for any hint of danger. When he caught a glimpse of a brown house between the trees, he signaled Teddy to stop as he dropped to a crouch. The dog sat by his side.

He watched the place for several long moments. There was no sign of anyone being nearby. Craning his neck, he searched for a vehicle, but didn't see one. Although from this angle, he couldn't see the west side of the house.

Was Lanier on the move? Or had he never been here at all?

He rose and took a circular path through the woods. He wanted to get closer to the house. Even from a distance, it looked beaten by the elements, faded wood, curling shingles. One of the dust-coated windows was broken.

Halfway around the house, a crack of gunfire echoed loudly. Chris hit the ground, covering Teddy with his body.

Lanier?

Without hesitation, he pulled out his phone and called for backup. Maybe it was a poacher, but he felt certain Lanier was hiding nearby.

"911. What's the nature of your emergency?" the dispatcher asked.

"I'm a K-9 officer with the Rocky Mountain K-9 Unit and just heard gunfire at what appears to be an abandoned property." He searched his memory for the address and rattled it off. "I need officers here ASAP!"

"I'll dispatch a unit right away."

Waiting wasn't his forte, so Chris gave Teddy the hand signal for sit, then retraced his steps, hoping to get to the front of the property. Before he'd gone ten feet, he heard the rumble of a car engine.

No! Lanier was getting away!

He put on a burst of speed, running through the woods even as he pulled his weapon. Crashing out of the brush, he caught a brief glimpse of the tail end of a dark pickup truck moving fast down the rutted driveway.

Wailing sirens echoed in the distance. Chris kept running after the truck, even though he sensed he was too late.

By the time he reached the road, there was no sign of the pickup truck. He ground his teeth together in frustration and called for Teddy. His partner quickly joined him.

The squad pulled up alongside him. A tall lanky cop emerged from behind the wheel. "I'm Officer Louis Howard. Did you report gunfire?"

"Yeah." Chris quickly explained what had transpired. "I don't know for sure the guy in the truck is Lanier, but it's a very strong possibility."

"Agree." Howard glanced at Teddy, then back at Chris. "Let's take a look around."

They went back to the abandoned house and found evidence of dust being disturbed, but no clear footprints. He offered Teddy the scent bag, but his K-9 didn't pick up Lanier's scent. Had the convict stayed in his vehicle the whole time? Maybe.

"Could have been some kids," Howard said. "We don't always have time to swing by to check the place out."

"I hear you." Still, he found it difficult to swallow

his frustration. He hadn't seen the truck at the house, but maybe Lanier had parked it out of view of the driveway. Once he and Teddy had gone around the house, the convict had taken the opportunity to fire a shot at him and escape.

"I'll let my fellow officers know of what happened here. We'll keep a closer eye on this place during our patrol rounds," Howard said when they'd finished searching the area.

"I appreciate that, thanks." Chris led Teddy to his SUV, watching as the lanky cop climbed back into his squad and drove away.

Glancing at his watch, he decided against finding the other property he'd identified. The one Lexie didn't know anything about. He'd come close to getting Lanier, but now he was anxious to return to the hangar. He wanted to be there when she arrived.

The drive didn't take long. Lexie's plane was still high in the sky, so he parked and took Teddy inside.

With Lexie's plane out of the structure, he had a better view of the two planes sitting farther back in the space. It made him wonder how often Harry, the owner, stopped in to take his planes out. So far, he hadn't seen the man over the past two days.

Teddy sniffed around the building, heading straight toward the smaller of the two planes. He saw Skip working near an open panel along the side of a Cessna.

"Skip?" he called out as he moved through the building.

"Who's there?" the mechanic snapped, whirling from the plane with wide eyes, holding a wrench up in a threatening manner. The older man's face flushed when he recognized Chris. "You shouldn't sneak up on an old man like that. You nearly gave me a heart attack."

"Sorry," he apologized. "I thought you saw me."

"Bah." Skip waved the wrench, muttering something Chris was glad he couldn't hear beneath his breath, before turning his attention back to the plane. No doubt he was replacing the fuel pump he'd mentioned yesterday.

Chris glanced around, wishing there was more security here. Sure, the hangar door was locked at night, but during the day, especially when Lexie was taking up tourists, the place was wide open.

It bothered him to know Lanier could sneak in at any time.

Spurred by this fear, Chris walked through the entire space, with Teddy at his side. Most of it was open, but there were storage containers. He looked behind fuel drums, and boxes of spare plane parts, verifying no one was hiding there. Finally, he was satisfied that Lanier wasn't hanging around, waiting to pounce.

Chris considered putting up some trail cameras around the hangar. They could be wired to a router that would connect with his phone and Lexie's, too. The kind he was familiar with only recorded when there was movement.

He'd need to run that idea past Lexie, who may need to ask the owner, but based on the break-in at her cabin, and the assault here in the hangar, he didn't think she'd mind. And he figured she could convince Harry, too.

Lexie's plane came closer, the twin engines growing louder as she approached the runway. Skip didn't seem to notice, his attention riveted on the fuel pump. Maybe the guy was hard of hearing. It would explain why the mechanic hadn't heard him and Teddy approach.

When Lexie's plane came rolling along the runway, Skip finally looked away from his work. The mechanic swiped his hands on the sides of his jeans, making black greasy smears as he walked over to the opening of the hangar.

Chris hung back, watching them. Then he frowned when he realized Teddy wasn't beside him.

"Teddy?" He called for the dog, but the sound of Lexie's plane made it difficult to be heard. A fission of anxiety hit as he walked around looking for his partner.

Normally, Teddy was trained to stay close to his side. The dog didn't wander off very often, and a chill snaked down his spine as he feared the worst.

"Teddy!" he shouted, louder this time.

His partner came out from beneath Skip's workbench. Chris frowned as the dog simply stood there, staring at him.

"What is it, boy?" He crossed over to where Teddy stood waiting. The minute he reached the animal's side, Teddy whirled and went back beneath the workbench.

And sat, looking up at him expectantly.

Teddy was alerting to Frank's scent, even without being told to seek. "Good boy," he praised, pulling out the small bear. Teddy jumped up and looked excited to have his prize. Chris tossed him the bear, then looked closer at the spot where Teddy had alerted.

There was a small garbage can that was empty except for one small scrap of paper. It looked as if it had been torn off from something larger.

Chris pulled an evidence bag from his pocket and used it as a glove to pick up the paper. There were four numbers written on it. One, one, one, eight.

He frowned. Had Lanier dropped this here? And if so, when? And more importantly, what did these numbers mean?

SIX

Lexie grinned as the four women gushed over their flight as they disembarked from the plane. There was nothing better than having satisfied customers.

For a brief time, she'd been able to put Frank Lanier's attacks behind her. Between the freedom of flying and her fun group, she hadn't given the smelly convict a second thought.

Finding Chris and Teddy waiting for her, though, was sobering. The grim expression on Chris's face indicated his search for Lanier hadn't been productive.

"Thanks again," she called as the four women left the hangar.

"Looks like they had a great time," Chris said with a smile.

"They did." She searched his gaze. "You didn't find anything at the abandoned property?"

"Someone, probably Lanier, took a shot at me and Teddy, but then got away. I only caught a glimpse of a dark pickup truck."

"He shot at you?" She gaped. "That's terrible."

"We're fine. I only wish I'd have gotten to him." He

shrugged. "I'll check out the other place I found this afternoon."

"He was using the place as a hideout."

"Maybe, but Teddy didn't pick up his scent anywhere, so either he stayed in his car the entire time, or the driver of the pickup truck was someone else."

The possibility that Lanier had stayed inside his car hadn't occurred to her. "Are you going to ask the police to stake the place out in case he is living out of his car?"

"Yes, Officer Louis Howard is going to have the police drive by more frequently. Great Falls might be the third-largest city in Montana, but the police force is small and stretched thin. They have acres and acres of land to cover out here. The good news is that every officer has Lanier's picture and are looking for him while out on patrol. We'll find him."

"I hope you're right." She blew out a breath, trying not to show her frustration. She couldn't believe how close Chris and Teddy had come to being injured, or worse. She sent up a silent prayer for God to continue watching over them, then she focused on Chris. "Now what?"

"I think you should go back to the motel until your afternoon tour."

She glanced over to where Skip was puttering with Harry's Cessna. "I would normally stick around here. I'd hate for something to happen to Skip."

"True." She thought Chris's gaze looked guarded. "But I'd like you to head back to the motel, anyway. At least for today. I'll feel better having you stashed someplace safe while Teddy and I continue searching for Lanier."

She hesitated, then nodded and turned toward her

cubicle office. "Okay, fine. Give me a few minutes to finish up my paperwork."

She made notes, then filed the flight plan and tour information. There had to be some way to convince Skip to head home until later this afternoon, too. Finding him at the hangar bright and early had been a surprise. What if Lanier had shown up?

Then again, she understood Skip wasn't necessarily in danger, at least not the way she was. Lanier clearly wanted her to fly him out of Great Falls. Why he'd targeted her, instead of any other pilot in the area, she had no idea. Maybe it was as simple as the fact she was one of the few female pilots. Easy prey, in his mind.

Glancing down at her computer, she was about to do another check-in on her father living back in New York, when she remembered her laptop was at the motel. The internet access was decent there, so she decided to look him up later.

Returning to the main hangar, she noticed Skip standing near Chris and Teddy, a deep scowl creasing his forehead.

"Don't see why I should have to suffer," the older man complained. "I got work to do here. Can't do that at home."

"Please do this for me, Skip," she said, hurrying over. "I'm sure this will all be over in a day or two at the most."

"Bah." Skip didn't look convinced and sent a narrow glare toward Chris. "Seems to me, that if your dog is as good as you say he is, this convict should have been caught already."

"Do you know Frank Lanier?" Chris asked.

Skip's scowl deepened. "No! Why would I know him?"

"I'm curious, that's all." The way Chris and Skip glared at each other was both concerning and confusing. "You seem more than willing to stay in the hangar alone despite a killer being on the loose."

"I can take care of myself." Skip huffed and abruptly headed toward his truck without saying another word. He climbed inside and slammed the door loud enough to make the old truck rattle.

Then he was gone.

She swung back to face Chris. "What was that about?"

"He's so stubborn, I needed a way to convince him that sticking around the hangar alone wasn't a good idea." He looked back toward the retreating vehicle for several long moments. "Mission accomplished."

"There must have been a nicer way to do that," she protested. "I know he's rather set in his ways, but Skip is a good mechanic, and he'd never cause anyone any harm."

Chris looked away, then gestured toward her Jeep. "I think you should park your vehicle inside the hangar."

She stared at him for a moment, wondering what he was thinking, before doing as he suggested. When that was finished, she closed and locked the hangar.

After putting Teddy in the back, and storing his pack, Chris opened her door for her. Once they were settled, she asked, "Are you going to look at that third property today?"

"That's the plan." He paused, then added, "I don't think you should get your hopes up, though. If Lanier is living in his car, he could be anywhere."

"Yeah." She tried not to feel depressed. "I wish there was a way to find him. Sooner than later."

"Me, too."

There was something off about Chris. Because of his recent close call? Maybe. She gazed out her window, searching for signs of Lanier, while trying to put her finger on what was different about him. He was acting reserved, as if he was holding something back.

She told herself it didn't matter. Chris was a cop. He was likely focused on finding Lanier, frustrated with the lack of progress the way she was.

Chris slowed the vehicle as they took a sharp curve in the road. Then he tapped the brakes. "Is that it?"

She craned her neck to see where he indicated. There was a post in the road with numbers on it, indicating there was an address for the property, but no sign of a clear driveway. "Maybe. But where is the driveway? I don't even see a clearing that could be used as one."

"I know. I'm thinking it could just be a parcel of land that isn't being used by anyone except for hunting." Chris released the brake and continued driving. "Teddy and I will check it out, but without access by car, I doubt it's being used as Lanier's hideout."

"Unless he's ditched the car and is going back and forth on foot," she pointed out.

"Maybe." Doubt laced his tone. "I don't really see Lanier as someone who has done a lot of hiking."

Remembering the stench of the guy's body odor, she could easily believe he wasn't used to physical activity. And was, in fact, likely living in his car. Then she frowned and turned in her seat to face him. "You mentioned Lanier was arrested for murder. Who did he kill?"

Chris didn't answer right away, making her wonder if it was some sort of secret.

"You don't have to tell me," she said.

"Lanier was arrested for murdering Brett Corea, the CEO of the largest bank in Helena. There was evidence that Corea was helping Lanier embezzle money. We believe Lanier wanted it all for himself and, based on his DNA found at the scene, took care of Corea to get him out of the way. Lanier also killed the deputy who was transporting him to his court hearing in Helena. Somehow, I can't imagine he's running around Great Falls on foot."

"That makes sense," she agreed.

Lanier's crimes made her think of her father, and the embezzling his business had done over the years. Her secret calls to the SEC had yet to yield results. She didn't understand why her father hadn't been arrested by now. How long did it take to build a case against him, anyway? It was strange, but there was nothing more she could do.

Yet the guilt of escaping New York to save herself still nagged at her. After her apartment had been broken into, she'd wasted no time in getting away from there.

But what if she'd stayed? What if she'd personally gone to the SEC with the information she'd found? Would her father already be behind bars?

She was so lost in her thoughts that she didn't realize Chris had pulled up in front of their adjoining motel rooms. She shook off the guilt, knowing it was too late to go back and change the past. God had brought her along this path for a reason. It wasn't up to her to question His will.

"Are you okay?" Chris asked.

"Fine." She forced a smile and pushed open her door. "Be safe."

"You, too." Chris didn't get out of the vehicle, but

she could feel his gaze on her as she unlocked the door and headed inside.

Telling herself the motel room wasn't a prison didn't help her feel better. She picked up her laptop and sat on her bed with her back against the headboard. Entering her father's name in the search engine, she stared at the same picture she'd found yesterday, of her father, her uncle Ron and the man campaigning to become the next mayor of New York.

No news wasn't necessarily good news. She closed the laptop and closed her eyes.

All she could do was pray.

Chris had no way of proving Skip was involved with Lanier. The scrap of paper with the weird numbers on it could have been left without Skip's knowledge. He'd watched the mechanic lose himself in his work. Plus, being hard of hearing meant Lanier could have sneaked in and out of the hangar without Skip knowing.

He needed to get the slip of paper to the team's tech guru, Russ Tate. He pulled over near the property he wanted to check out and called him.

"Tate," Russ answered.

"Hey, it's Chris. Listen, I found a slip of paper in the garbage can in a small hangar with the numbers one, one, one, eight written on it. It might be related to Frank Lanier. Do those numbers mean anything to you concerning him or his case?"

"Not off the bat. It could be all sorts of things," Russ pointed out. "Numbers of a combination lock, although those are generally three digits, not four. Could be part of a license plate. A phone number. Or a safe-deposit box."

Chris grimaced and ran his hand over his closely

cropped black hair. "You're right, there are too many possibilities."

"Are you sure those numbers are related to your case?" Russ asked.

"Teddy alerted on the slip of paper, so it has Frank Lanier's scent on it."

"Oh, well, then I can see if I can come up with any leads as far as license plates go," Russ offered.

"Thanks. I'll send this to you as soon as I can. I'd like you to check for possible fingerprints."

"Okay. Anything else?"

"Nothing new on the boot print found in the woods?"

"No, it's a common brand sold all over the country."

That figured. He swallowed his disappointment. "Thanks for trying. I'll be in touch soon."

"Roger that." Russ disconnected from the line.

Chris slid out from behind the wheel and pocketed his phone. He grabbed his pack and let Teddy out. He checked the K-9's vest before he smiled down at his partner. "Ready to work, boy?"

Teddy waved his tail.

Chris offered him the scent bag and then commanded him to seek. Teddy lifted his nose, sniffing the air before trotting down the road a few yards. When Teddy jumped the ditch and disappeared through the foliage, Chris quickly followed.

He wasn't sure what had caught Teddy's attention; there was no path nearby. He'd spent enough time in the wilderness to recognize the signs of broken branches or trampled greenery.

"Teddy!" A flicker of unease washed over him. "Teddy, come!"

He came out of the woods to a small clearing, where

Teddy stood waiting for him. After making sure Chris was paying attention, Teddy went over to a large boulder and sat, staring up at him.

"Frank was here, huh? Good boy." He pulled the bear out of his pocket and tossed it to the spaniel. Then he searched the area for clues.

No boot prints. The ground was dry, and he realized the scent could be several days old. Lanier may have been here before the thunderstorm had washed away the evidence.

Chris gently took the stuffed bear away from Teddy and pulled out the scent bag again. The dog instantly looked alert. "Seek! Seek Frank."

Teddy whirled, putting his nose to the ground this time. As his partner went on the move, Chris was excited to see there was a path. Not much of one, but enough to indicate Lanier must have come this way on foot.

Teddy set a fast pace, forcing Chris to keep up. Sweat trickled down the back of his neck, dampening his shirt. He didn't ask the dog to slow down, though, because he needed to finish investigating this lead before it was time to return to the motel and drive Lexie back to the hangar.

Following Teddy, Chris estimated they'd only gone about five yards when he saw the dirt road.

His partner alerted near the edge of the road. He quickly tossed the bear in the air for Teddy to catch, then looked for more boot prints. He found a partial and used his phone to take a picture. Pulling up the previous photos, he could tell they were the same.

Clearly Lanier had driven along the dirt road to this location. He'd gotten out, then had taken the path through the woods, maybe hoping to find a dwelling. The hike had been rather long, though. Based on how out of shape the guy was, Chris would have assumed Lanier would have given up over halfway along the journey.

Unless he'd been here for some other reason?

Two vehicles could have met here, he supposed. The dirt road was packed down and grown over with weeds, making it impossible to distinguish a decent tire tread.

Yet who could have met up with Lanier? Skip Taylor? Some other accomplice? Difficult to imagine that Skip had helped Frank escape from the prison transport van.

But someone else had.

He scowled, remembering the glimpse of the pickup truck he'd seen. Lanier? Or his accomplice?

This case was making his head hurt. He lightly touched the bruise on his temple. The souvenir he'd received from Lanier less than twenty-four hours ago.

Twenty-four hours too long, he thought grimly.

Glancing at his watch, he winced. He was running out of time, but he really wanted to figure out where this road went. Chris pulled out his GPS and reviewed a map of the area in his mind. He decided the dirt road had to lead to the main highway at some point. Hopefully, close to where he'd left his SUV.

"Come, Teddy."

The spaniel dropped the bear at his feet. Chris slid it back into his pack and then strode purposefully down the road. Teddy trotted beside him. Chris liked having a four-legged partner, although there were times he wished Teddy could talk things through with him.

Like discussing the complexities of this case.

The urge to call Ben was strong. His brother would

understand and share his frustration. The road curved around a particularly large tree. He went through two large overgrown bushes and found the highway. As he'd suspected, it was only about sixty yards from where he'd left his SUV.

He placed Teddy in the back, and slid behind the wheel, cranking the air-conditioning. He didn't have much time, but instead of heading back to the motel, he turned onto the dirt road.

Just a few miles, he promised himself. He wanted to go just far enough to have an idea where the road might end.

The SUV bumped and rolled over the uneven earth beneath the wheels. He ticked the miles off in his head and was about to turn around when he saw something flash between a break in the trees.

A building? He continued moving forward, coming to an abrupt stop when he realized where he was.

He was looking at the back side of a building. One that looked familiar. He stared in shock.

It was the Blue Skye Aviation hangar.

SEVEN

Lexie paced the length of the motel room, growing more frustrated by the minute. Chris was late and she was stranded here without her Jeep. She'd called him, but the phone went to voice mail, likely because he was in an area without decent cell coverage.

A common occurrence in Montana.

But her mind kept going back to the recent gunfire. What if Lanier had killed Chris and Teddy? She didn't want to think the worst, but it was difficult not to worry. Chris was an experienced cop. She needed to have faith in his ability, and Teddy's, too.

A more likely explanation was that Teddy had picked up Lanier's scent, taking Chris farther into the woods. The pair had likely lost track of time.

She appreciated Chris's desire to keep her safe, but he'd promised to be back in time to drive her back to the hangar for her one-thirty tour. Not that she wanted to interfere with his investigation, but still.

Next time, she'd make sure she had her own set of wheels.

Glancing at her watch, she grimaced. She'd give him another fifteen minutes, then call for a rideshare. Lexie was about to try Chris one more time when her phone rang. Recognizing Chris's number, she let out a small sigh of relief.

"I'm on my way," he said quickly before she could express her frustration. "Sorry about the delay, but I'll fill you in when I get there."

"Okay." She barely had time to respond before he cut off from the call. Thankfully, he was all right. And she felt a surge of anticipation that Chris and Teddy may have found something worthwhile.

After booting up her computer, she double-checked the weather forecast. The wind had kicked up a bit since earlier that morning, but not enough to cancel her tour.

True to his word, Chris pulled in ten minutes later. She didn't hesitate to rush out of the motel and jump into the passenger seat. "I was worried sick something happened to you," she said as she buckled in. "I'm glad you're okay, and that you made it here. I was just about to call for a rideshare."

"I know, I'm sorry. Teddy tracked Lanier's scent through the woods of that abandoned property." He glanced at her, his topaz gaze serious. "The trail took us to a dirt road."

"A dirt road?" She frowned. "I'm not familiar with a road in that location."

"Well, you should know the dirt road leads to the back of your hangar."

She blinked. "What? How is that possible? I mean, why would there be a road back there?" She couldn't imagine why anyone would have created that sort of access. Especially since the main highway came right up to the parking lot.

"I'm not sure. I plan to look at it more closely after

you're safely in the air." He frowned. "But I have to say, the road is not being used frequently. It's really grown over."

"Maybe that's why I never noticed it from the plane." She stared out the windshield for a long moment. "You think Lanier used that road to drive up to the hangar?"

"Yeah, I do. It explains why we didn't see his vehicle anywhere in the area." He shrugged. "I took Teddy back that way, but we never made it all the way to the road, which is my fault."

"Don't." She lightly touched his arm, concerned at his self-deprecating tone. "You've been doing everything possible to find him, Chris. You risked your life to rescue me, twice."

He didn't answer, his jaw appearing to be set in stone. She dropped her hand, not understanding why he was being so hard on himself. Glancing over her shoulder, she looked at Teddy, who was stretched out in the crated area of the SUV. She smiled when he thumped his tail in recognition. He was a great dog, and she was glad Chris had him as a partner.

"Can I see the road?" she asked.

"Not a good idea. I haven't fully investigated the area yet." He glanced over at her. "Try to trust me on this."

"I do trust you," she hastened to assure him. "More than I've trusted anyone in a very long time."

A true statement, since she hadn't been able to trust anyone in her family. Not her parents, her uncle, her brother, not even her friends.

She'd made a few friendships here in Great Falls, but none that she considered especially close. Keeping secrets tended to prevent that.

Which only made her feel guilty about the secrets she was keeping from Chris.

"Thanks, Lexie." His features softened slightly. "How many are in your tour group this afternoon?"

"A foursome—parents, a grandparent and a five-year-old boy." She grimaced. "Hopefully the youngster will do okay. It's not common that people pay this kind of money for a kid that age to fly over the Rocky Mountains. I doubt he'll remember this experience when he's older."

"But his parents will, which might be all that matters." Chris spoke absently, his attention on the road and the traffic behind them.

They arrived at the hangar with just a few minutes to spare before her tour group showed up. Thankfully, Skip was already there, checking over the bird. He helped her pull the plane out just as a car pulled into the small parking lot.

"Just in time," she murmured, pasting a smile on her face to greet her guests. "Welcome to Blue Skye Aviation. My name is Lexie McDaniels, and I'm your pilot and tour guide for today."

Bobby, the five-year-old, hopped around the parking lot in a way that made her wonder if he would be able to sit still throughout the tour. Trying not to sigh, she led the group over to the plane and helped them inside.

Chris and Teddy stood off to the side, keeping out of the way. She knew the moment she was in the air, the pair would go back to searching for the dirt road that apparently came up to the back of her hangar.

She slid into the pilot's seat and pulled her headphones on. Then she went through her preflight checklist, noting with satisfaction that Skip had topped off the fuel tank.

"Ready?" she asked as she started the engines.

"Faster, go faster," Bobby shouted.

"Okay, here we go." She gathered speed as she headed toward the runway. Just like they had earlier that morning, she noticed Chris and Teddy watching from the ground just outside the hangar, not taking their eyes off her until she lifted the bird into the air. She couldn't afford to let their mission distract her from her job, so she focused on doing what she could.

Please watch over them, Lord.

Once Lexie was in the air, Chris turned to Skip. "What's with the dirt road behind the hangar?"

"Huh?" There was a flash of guilt in the older man's eyes before he turned away. "Don't know nothing about that."

"I think you do." Chris followed the mechanic as he headed toward his workbench. "And believe me, I'll hold you to the full extent of the law if I find out you're helping Lanier escape."

"I'm not." This time, the old man turned to face him. "I care about Lexie."

Chris stared at him for a long moment, wondering if he could believe him. "Then what's with the dirt road?"

Skip shrugged. "I think it's been there for years," he finally admitted. "I don't know anything about it because it doesn't go anywhere. No one uses it."

Not true, because Frank had driven on it. He narrowed his gaze. "Why is it even there, then? It must have been used for something at one point."

Skip turned back to his workbench. "I think the

owner of that plot of land on the other side of the hangar used it to access his property. Last I heard, the guy gave up his idea of building a house back there and relocated back to California."

Chris wanted to believe Skip, but the way the old man dodged his initial question made him wonder if the mechanic knew more than he was willing to share.

But why would Skip keep his association with Lanier a secret? That part didn't make any sense. Lanier may have offered money, but he obviously didn't have any cash on him. Unless he'd robbed someone along the way.

Anything was possible. And the scrap of paper Teddy had found in the wastebasket beneath Skip's workbench was part of the puzzle.

Hopefully, Russ would get back to him about those numbers soon. He'd stopped at a delivery service in town to send the evidence to Russ, paying an exorbitant fee to have it arrive within twenty-four hours.

A side trip that had made him even later to pick up Lexie.

"Come, Teddy." Chris turned and led the way outside the hangar. He estimated the general location of the dirt road, before unclipping Teddy's leash. He pulled the scent bag from his pack, offered it to the dog and gave the command. "Seek!"

Teddy eagerly set out through the woods, following the general path he'd taken the previous day. Teddy found the boot print again, so he rewarded the dog and gave him a brief water break before putting him back to work.

Teddy trotted through the woods, his nose constantly working as he searched for Frank's scent. Chris gamely kept pace with his partner, ignoring the sweat trickling down his spine and making his shirt stick to his back.

It wasn't until Teddy alerted at the base of a tree that he could see they were close to the dirt road. He rewarded his partner, then glanced around with a frown. If this road had been created to access the hangar, shouldn't there be some sort of path?

If so, Frank hadn't used it.

They kept going until they were back out on the road. Earlier, he hadn't gone any farther than the hangar, but now he continued following the road. Teddy didn't alert on Frank's scent, but that wasn't a surprise if the guy had left a vehicle back there.

He estimated they'd gone another two hundred yards before the road abruptly stopped. With a frown, he turned and looked back the way they'd come. How strange that the road went absolutely nowhere.

Just like Skip had said.

From this section of the road, the woods had thinned to the point there weren't many trees, providing a decent view of the runway. Surely this wasn't the spot where the property owner had intended to build a house.

Dejected that he hadn't found anything useful, he turned to head back to the hangar. But then he hesitated and offered the scent bag to Teddy once again. Maybe Frank had parked somewhere else along this road, or had come out of the woods someplace else.

His partner eagerly began to sniff the area. Teddy didn't alert until the area where they'd originally come out of the woods. "Good boy," he praised, offering the stuffed bear.

They trudged through the woods back to the hangar. Chris ignored the rumbling of his stomach reminding him he'd missed lunch, and the longing for a shower and change of clothes. He walked Teddy through the hangar, hoping his partner might find something more.

Like the paper in the wastebasket.

Unfortunately, Teddy didn't alert on anything else. Disappointing, although not a surprise.

Skip's head was buried in the Cessna again. "I thought you fixed the fuel pump?"

"Gotta get the air out of the fuel line." Skip's voice was muffled.

Chris wondered if there was truly enough work here to keep the mechanic busy day in and day out. Was it possible lack of money had enticed him to secretly help Lanier? What if the convict was right now hiding at Skip's place?

He narrowed his gaze, watching the older man for several minutes. Then he turned and glanced out at Skip's beat-up truck sitting in the lot.

"Come, Teddy." He led the dog back outside, directly over to Skip's truck. "Seek Frank."

The dog obediently sniffed the ground near the driver's side door, then circled the vehicle, raising his nose to test the air.

Nothing.

Moving to the passenger side door, Chris pulled the handle, expecting the truck to be locked.

It wasn't. "Seek Frank," he said in a low tone.

Teddy nosed around the interior of the pickup truck again, without alerting. Chris quickly closed the door and moved away from the battered pickup truck before Skip could ask what he was doing.

Okay, so maybe the mechanic hadn't given Lanier a ride, but that alone wasn't enough for Chris to let him off the hook. He made a mental note to have Teddy check out the area around Skip's house later that afternoon.

Once Lexie was safe.

He headed over to his SUV, opening the back for Teddy. He started the vehicle to activate the freshwater system, allowing Teddy to drink.

Sitting on the rear bumper of the SUV, he heard the distant sound of Lexie's plane approaching. For her sake, he hoped the little boy hadn't tossed his cookies during the flight.

She was a bit of an enigma, extremely smart and self-reliant, yet content to run her small tourist business. Not that there was anything wrong with that, but he didn't think she'd lived here in Montana her entire life. Every once in a while, he caught a hint of an East Coast accent in her voice.

This curiosity about Lexie wasn't healthy or normal. Since the fiasco with Debra, he hadn't been interested in heading down that road again. Especially since his job was one that did require travel. Their Rocky Mountain K-9 Unit offered assistance through a variety of states. Montana was the farthest he'd been over the past few months, but he figured he'd be back again at some point.

Not that he planned to stop in to see Lexie again. Nope. No more long-distance relationships, no matter how much he liked her. He was here to do a job, and when he had Lanier in custody, he'd never see her again.

Why did that thought depress him?

Lexie's plane grew larger as she dropped her altitude in preparation to land. He watched with a sense of awe as she deftly brought the plane level to the ground, then slowly touched down.

She drove the plane to the front of the hangar, stopping just short to allow her passengers to get out. As she jumped down from the cockpit, he sensed she looked a bit frazzled.

"I hope you enjoyed your flight," she said as she helped her passengers off the plane.

"We did, right, Bobby?" The younger woman he assumed was Bobby's mother grabbed a hold of the little boy's hand. "Again, I'm really sorry about the headphones."

"Don't worry about it," Lexie said with a pained smile. "I'm glad you had fun."

"Thanks again." Bobby's father waved as he ushered the group to their car.

Chris closed his SUV and walked toward Lexie. "What happened?"

"Bobby broke his headphones." She sighed. "It's fine, though. I have plenty of spares."

"At least he didn't get sick."

That made her smile. "I know, right? Could have been worse. Did you find anything?"

"No, the road basically dead-ends." He shrugged. "At least we know it's not used very often."

She nodded, then reached inside the plane, pulling out the broken headphones. "Give me a few minutes. I'll be back shortly."

"Okay." He stayed where he was, glancing back at Skip's truck. He really wanted to head over to the mechanic's house, and didn't necessarily want to waste time in driving Lexie back to the motel.

As he mulled over his options, Skip surprised him by coming to stand beside him. The mechanic pulled a crumpled pack of filterless cigarettes from his shirt pocket and lit one up.

"I was thinking about that property over yonder," Skip said after taking a long drag off his cigarette.

"What about it?"

"Think I remember hearing the guy who owned the place was Joe Palmer." He wrinkled his forehead. "Used to own this hangar, too."

"Really?" Chris straightened upon hearing that tidbit of information. "When I searched the property records, his name didn't show up."

"Huh, that's strange." Skip took another hit off the cigarette. "Maybe he defaulted on paying his property taxes so the land went back to the state. Or maybe Harry bought that land, too, along with the hangar. Harry has owned the hangar for the past fifteen years."

He remembered learning that Harry Olson owned the hangar and the two planes that he'd yet to see in the air. He pinned Skip with a narrow look. "I'd like Harry's phone number if you have it." For all he knew, the last four digits of the owner's phone number were one-one-one-eight.

"Yeah, sure." Skip nodded thoughtfully, patting his pockets. "My phone is inside. But you know, I think I remember hearing that Joe Palmer was the one who put in that road, you know, as a way to connect the properties."

"That makes sense." He thought it was odd that the mechanic was suddenly chatty, when earlier he hadn't even wanted to admit to knowing anything about the road.

Teddy growled low in his throat, his nose pointed at the hangar. Teddy was trained not to growl at strangers, but in that moment, Chris realized Lexie was inside the hangar, alone.

Was this why Skip had come outside to smoke?

"Lexie!" He shouted her name as he burst into a run.

EIGHT

"I need that money, and you're going to get it for me," Frank whispered in her ear. Lexie tried to breathe around the tight hold around her neck, silently praying for Skip or Chris to come rescue her. Then Frank abruptly thrust her forward with enough force that she couldn't keep herself from falling onto the concrete floor.

"Lexie!" Chris shouted her name again. Her knees and her hands throbbed in pain, but she managed to lift her head, looking around the far corner of the hangar. "Where are you?"

"Here," she croaked. She pushed herself upright, wincing as her bruised muscles protested.

She saw Chris making his way toward her, going around Harry's two planes, the Cessna and the Beechcraft, with Teddy at his side. He rushed forward to help her up off the floor. "What happened? Are you okay?"

"Lanier," she said, rubbing her bruised throat. She'd smelled him seconds before he'd come out of the shadows, grabbing and choking her before she could cry out for help. "He was here."

Chris looked around the hangar. "Where did he go?"

"There's a rear door." She gestured toward it, then smiled when Teddy licked her bruised knee. "It's hard to see because it's near those fuel drums. Honestly, we rarely use it."

He stared at the door along the back wall, his expression grim. "Now I know how he's getting in and out of here. We need to lock that door, ASAP."

"Okay, I can ask Skip to do that."

"No, I'll take care of it. But first, I need to get you someplace safe. No way am I leaving you here alone with Skip."

She frowned. "Why not?"

He hesitated, then said, "Why wasn't Skip in here when you needed him? He's always tinkering with the plane engines. Until the moment you were attacked by Lanier. You went in to get new headphones and suddenly Skip is outside chatting with me while smoking a cigarette. Before today, the guy barely spoke in complete sentences."

It took a moment for his observation to sink in. "I— don't understand. Skip wouldn't have any reason to help Lanier or to hurt me."

"I don't trust him." Chris's tone didn't invite an argument. "I need to get you back to the motel."

"First we need to talk to Skip," she protested. "I'm sure there's a logical reason why he came out of the hangar when he did." She couldn't wrap her mind around the idea that the mechanic she'd worked with over the past five years was capable of such a thing.

"Yes, let's talk to him." Chris slipped his arm around her waist and she gratefully leaned against him. She swallowed a moan, unwilling to let on how much she hurt. There wasn't anything that could be done for her bruises other than taking over-the-counter pain meds.

Still, her progress through the hangar was slow. By the time they were outside, there was no sign of Skip or his battered truck.

"He's in on this," Chris muttered harshly. "I wish I had more evidence that he's involved so I could arrest him for his role in Lanier's assaulting you."

She couldn't see how Skip could be held accountable for what had nearly happened in the hangar. "Maybe you should take Teddy out and search for Lanier instead."

"I would, but I can't leave you alone." Chris sighed. "Besides, I'm sure Lanier had a vehicle waiting on the dirt road behind the hangar. He's probably long gone by now."

"I never expected him to show up during the daytime." She glanced around the area, wondering if she'd ever feel safe here again. "Lanier must be getting desperate."

"What did he say?"

She hesitated. He'd mentioned needing "the money." But what money? She certainly didn't have any. Although her father did.

Was that what this was about? Could Lanier really be connected with her dad's crimes? But how? Helena, Montana, was a long way from New York City.

"He said something about needing money," she finally admitted. "And that I was going to get it for him."

"You?" Chris hiked an eyebrow. "Why?"

She shook her head. "It must be that he needs to get somewhere that is only accessible by plane."

Chris's expression turned thoughtful. "He was arrested and charged with embezzling money. Could be he or someone else stashed it nearby."

"Stashed it, how? By using another plane? I can assure you I didn't take anyone out for a tour to hide money. I don't like landing in unfamiliar terrain." She thought about Harry Olson, the owner of Blue Skye Aviation. "I guess Harry may have taken someone out without realizing what was going on."

"That's a really good idea, Lexie. Do you have access to his flight records?" Chris asked.

"We can check Harry's office. He's still away visiting his daughter and new grandson in Billings." She wasn't thrilled about snooping around her boss's stuff, but there was no doubt in her mind that Lanier wasn't going to rest until he'd gotten his flight out of here.

And maybe that's why he targeted her to be his pilot. Because Harry might recognize him and ask too many questions.

Yet her thoughts kept coming back to his comment about money.

Cash he'd embezzled from wealthy ranchers? Or money he thought was owed to him because it had been stolen through one of her father's Ponzi schemes? Had Lanier once been one of her father's clients? Those clients were located across the country. But even if that was the case, Lanier would have no way of knowing who she was.

"Lexie?" Chris's voice held concern.

She forced a smile. "I'm fine. Let's go."

With Lexie appreciating Chris's support, they moved through the hangar to the opposite side of the building. Harry's office was much larger than her cubicle space, with a door that locked. Thankfully, Harry didn't bother with locking the place, likely due to the fact there was nothing of value in there. Flight plans and customer lists wouldn't be targeted by a thief.

She entered the room, trying to ignore how she was about to invade her boss's privacy. She sank into Harry's chair and opened his file drawer. The file folders were not listed in alphabetical order, which made her wonder if he'd bothered to keep detailed flight records the way she did.

"What can I do to help?" Chris asked.

She glanced up at the file drawer. "Board up that back door. I'm sure I'll be fine here."

He hesitated, then glanced at his partner. "I'll have Teddy stay here with you. Sit, Teddy. Stay."

The dog sat on command. She smiled as Teddy's dark brown eyes followed Chris's progress as he left the office to grab some tools from Skip's workbench.

Skip. She was dumbfounded that the mechanic might be involved in this. Her gaze landed on a file folder titled "Repairs." She pulled it out and skimmed through the documents inside.

She found an invoice for a tire that had needed to be replaced a few days ago. Frowning, she tried to think back to that time frame. She didn't recall Harry mentioning any damage to his plane.

The most common way a tire went flat was during a crash landing. Or landing on rocky terrain. She put the invoice aside, wondering if there was significance to the timing of the repair. The tire would have gone flat the same day as Lanier's escape from the prison van.

A coincidence? Maybe.

She continued poking through Harry's files with

Teddy sitting beside her. She listened as Chris pounded and hammered the rear door shut.

When he'd finished, she hadn't found anything else identifying who Harry had taken up in that plane ride when the tire had gone flat. She showed him the invoice. "This could have happened if Harry made an unscheduled landing, but I can't find any other evidence proving that theory."

He took the invoice, nodding slowly. "This could help, thanks. No way of knowing where this happened?"

She waved at the messy files. "I have found some flight plans, but not very many. I'm surprised by that, though. It's almost as if Harry gave up keeping track of them. He doesn't take tours up as often as he used to."

"Okay." He scowled and carefully folded the invoice and tucked it away. "Thanks for trying."

She pushed herself to her feet, wincing as her sore knees protested. She'd landed on them twice now, and could really feel it.

"Hey, are you okay?" Chris must have noticed her discomfort, because he came over to stand beside her. "You need a cold pack."

She took a step and nearly buckled as pain shot down her leg. He quickly wrapped his arms around her and pulled her against him. "Whoa, easy now. Let me help you."

She couldn't help looping her arms around his waist, breathing in his musky scent. Being held by Chris was making her dizzy in a different way. A reaction to his nearness. Walking seemed impossible, but she told herself to buck up and get it done.

Only she didn't move.

"Lexie," he whispered, running a hand down her back. "I'm so sorry you've been hurt."

"It's not your fault." Her voice was muffled by his shirt. She tipped her head back to look up at him. "I want him found and arrested as much as you do."

"I know." Chris gazed down into her eyes for a long moment. He reached up and tucked a strand of her dark wavy hair behind her ear. His mouth was so close…

He kissed her. Gently, at first, then with a sense of urgency that robbed her of the ability to think. It had been so long since a man had held her, kissed her.

Protected her.

She gripped him tightly, desperately wishing their embrace didn't have to end.

Chris lifted his head, his breathing choppy and his mind spinning from the impact of kissing Lexie.

How was it possible she'd knocked him so far off kilter? He had to force himself to loosen his grip. "I—uh, sorry."

"Don't be." Was it his imagination or was there a flash of hurt in her green eyes? He honestly couldn't say he was sorry for kissing her, only that he'd taken advantage of the situation.

Dude, keep your head in the game and stay focused on the case.

"I'm fine." The way Lexie avoided his direct gaze was not convincing. He hated knowing he might have hurt her. "Um, so where to, now?"

"Let's get you out to the SUV." He kept his arm around her for support, and maybe because he wasn't quite ready to let her go, while doing his best to ignore her lilac scent.

"I need to lock up," she protested, pulling away from him. He reluctantly let her go, watching with concern as she moved slowly to the hangar's overhead garage door.

"Wait, shouldn't we put your Jeep inside?" he asked.

"No, I'm driving it." She glanced at him over her shoulder, then quickly looked away. "I don't want to be stranded at the motel again."

"But you don't have any more tours today, do you?" He didn't like the idea of her driving the Jeep. Then again, keeping the Jeep inside the hangar wasn't necessarily a good option, either. He'd boarded up the back door, but there was a window in both offices. Lanier could easily break in to steal the Jeep.

Or sabotage it.

"No, I don't have any more tours, but I'm taking my Jeep," she repeated firmly.

He rubbed his hand over his short hair. "Okay, fine. But you stay close, okay?"

Lexie nodded and quickly locked the hangar door. "We're heading to Skip's house, right?"

That was his plan, but he didn't want Lexie tagging along. "Let's go to the motel, first. After you're safe, I'll head out to his place."

"No." Lexie's green eyes flashed with unmistakable stubbornness. "I know Skip. He'll open up to me."

He stared at her. Didn't she understand the guy had all but handed her over to Lanier? He firmly believed Skip was involved in this mess. "I don't think so. It's my job to find Lanier and to keep you safe."

"I know where he lives." Lexie used her key fob to unlock her Jeep and headed toward it. "You can follow me or meet up with me there. But I'm going."

Chris lifted his gaze to the sky, struggling to rein in

his frustration. Maybe once he would have prayed for strength and wisdom.

But not anymore.

"Come, Teddy." He didn't see any choice but to follow her to Skip's house. He placed Teddy inside, stored his backpack, then slid behind the wheel. Thankfully, Lexie waited for him, before driving out of the parking lot.

Chris kept Lexie's taillights in view as they made their way down the highway. He wondered if Skip would even be there, or if the mechanic had headed into town. For all he knew, this could be a wasted trip.

Which was actually the better option. At least that way he might be able to get Lexie back to the motel without putting her in any more danger.

He berated himself for not figuring out that Skip was distracting him on purpose, until it was almost too late. If it wasn't for Teddy's growling—he swallowed hard, unwilling to finish that thought. Bad enough that Lexie had been hurt again. All because Lanier wanted her to fly him out to where the money was stashed. Or so they believed.

No surprise Lanier had an accomplice; it was something he'd suspected all along. The big question was who'd helped him? As much as he believed Skip was involved with Lanier now, he couldn't imagine the older man helping to break the convict out of jail.

Unless he'd seriously underestimated the guy.

The accomplice must have known the route the prison van was scheduled to take. He made a mental note to ask Lexie if Skip had been gone for any length of time. Although he thought it likely she'd have mentioned that earlier.

Especially after finding the invoice for the flat tire.

Lexie's Jeep slowed as she took a corner. He followed, noting the area was deserted.

Much like Lexie's cabin had been.

His shoulders tensed as he raked his gaze over their surroundings. If they didn't find Skip here at his house, he planned to take Teddy out to search for Frank's scent. If Lanier had been there, he'd have more evidence of Skip's culpability in aiding and abetting a known felon.

He'd cuff the mechanic and haul him to jail faster than he could blink.

Finally Lexie turned onto a barely visible gravel driveway. He followed, his SUV rocking and rolling over the rutted earth. When she stopped, he slammed on the brake, shut off his car and jumped out before she could move.

"Stay here for a minute," he said tersely. "We could be walking into an ambush."

"I doubt it. I don't see Skip's truck." Lexie peered through the windshield. "It doesn't look like anyone is home."

"Maybe, but I'm armed and you're not. So give me some time here to look around." Chris wasn't willing to risk Teddy yet, either, not until he'd made sure there was no one hiding inside with a weapon trained on them.

Lexie's point about not seeing Skip's truck, or any other vehicle for that matter, was a good one. But he wasn't about to take a risk.

Not with Teddy or Lexie.

He pulled his weapon from his holster and moved up to Skip's cabin. The place was smaller and more weather-beaten than Lexie's, giving him the impression that Skip had lived here a long time.

Was the mechanic in debt to the bank? Was that why he'd helped Lanier get to Lexie?

He peered through the window, looking at a messy kitchen. No sign of anyone, so he moved on to the next. It wasn't until he reached the third window looking into the living room that he paused and swallowed hard.

Booted feet poked out from behind the sofa.

Skip's feet? Most likely. Still, he didn't know if Lanier was hiding out in there, so he continued making his way around the house.

When he didn't see anyone else lurking inside, he returned to the front. He gestured to the door as a way of informing Lexie what he was going to do.

That someone was lying on the floor inside provided him the exigent circumstances he needed. The front door was locked, no surprise, so he kicked it with his foot. Two solid kicks and the wood around the doorjamb splintered, allowing the door to swing open.

Leading with his gun, Chris cautiously moved into the cabin. "Skip? It's the police. Come out with your hands where I can see them."

No answer. Not that he'd expected one.

Moving closer, he grimaced when he recognized Skip lying on the floor, blood staining the man's chest. He'd been shot at close range. Chris didn't offer aid, though, until he'd cleared the rest of the house, making sure Lanier wasn't hiding nearby.

When he returned to the living room, he scowled when he saw Lexie kneeling beside Skip.

"Skip, it's Lexie. Can you hear me? Open your eyes, Skip."

He came over to knee beside her. "Does he have a pulse?"

"Yes, but it's very faint." Lexie's eyes held concern. "I've called for an ambulance, but I'm afraid they'll be too late. We shouldn't have waited so long, Chris. If Skip dies..." Her voice trailed off.

He didn't argue, because while keeping the hangar safe had seemed like a priority, he should have considered the possibility of Lanier meeting up with Skip and silencing the guy so he couldn't talk.

Guilt flailed at him. Why was he always a step behind Lanier?

Skip groaned and stirred. Chris bent over, gently turning the man's head to face him. "Skip, what happened? Who did this to you? Was it Lanier?"

Skip's eyelids fluttered open, but his gaze was unfocused. He let out another moan, and mumbled, "He wants—Lexie..."

"Who wants her? Frank Lanier? Why?" Chris tightened his grip on the man's shoulder. "Come on, Skip. Tell us what happened."

"Sorry, Lex..." Skip's eyes drifted shut and his body went slack.

"No! Skip!" Lexie cried. "Hang on. The ambulance will be here soon!"

But as Chris felt for his pulse, he knew it was already too late.

Skip was dead.

NINE

Tears rolled down her cheeks as she watched the ambulance crew lift Skip's body from the floor to place him on the gurney. There was no urgency in their movements, as he was dead. Though she knew the guy was more than capable of such a horrific act, she was shocked that he'd killed Skip.

They should have gotten here sooner.

Chris was speaking with the local police who'd accompanied the ambulance to the scene. His expression was grim, and she knew guilt was weighing on him.

She swiped at her eyes and dropped her chin to her chest in an effort to maintain her composure.

Lanier was responsible for three murders now. Brett Corea, the deputy in the transport van and Skip.

How many others? Maybe people they didn't even know about yet?

As much as she wished she could go back and change the past, she knew they had to keep moving forward. To understand why Lanier was so determined to get to her.

It was difficult to acknowledge that Chris had been right. That Skip had set her up to be grabbed by Lanier.

For money? Or had he been threatened in order to get him to cooperate?

To her knowledge, Skip didn't have any family nearby. She gave herself a shake and tried to pull herself together. Skip's murder changed things. It was more important than ever to find Lanier. Before he found her.

Again.

Chris crossed over and put his hand on her shoulder. "I'm so sorry, Lexie. It's my fault."

"No, it's not," she swiftly countered. "Lanier did this. And you were right. Skip purposefully left me in the hangar alone so Lanier could grab me."

Chris looked as if he carried the weight of the world on his shoulders. "I should have anticipated this. Maybe if we had come straight here…"

"We don't know when Lanier arrived," she reminded him. "Skip probably bolted from the hangar the minute you left him to come inside. And Skip's truck isn't here, so maybe Skip picked up Lanier along the way. We may still have been too late."

Chris blew out a heavy sigh. "You're being too nice about this, far more than I deserve."

Her heart squeezed in empathy. She reached up to cover his hand with hers. "You've saved my life several times, Chris. I'm very grateful. Please know God is watching over us."

He looked away. "I'm not sure about that."

"I am." She smiled, wishing there was a way to convince him. "Please have faith in Him. God is guiding us on this path, Chris. I truly believe we'll find Lanier."

"Before he kills again?" Chris winced, then amended, "Sorry, I clearly need an attitude adjustment."

She moved closer, slipping her arm around his waist. "I could use a hug."

He wrapped his arms around her and held her close for several long moments. She wished he'd kiss her again, but was content to soak in his strength.

His courage.

"Okay, I think it's time Teddy and I went to work," he said, easing away. "First I'll follow you back to the motel."

"No, I want to come with you." She wasn't about to sit around doing nothing. "Please, Chris. It's important to me that we find him."

The scowl on his face indicated he wasn't buying into her idea.

"There's no point in wasting time," she added. "Maybe he left in a rush, leading to his making a mistake."

"I'd rather have one of the local cops watching over you."

"They're a small police force and already watching for Lanier," she protested. "That would be a waste of resources."

He frowned but seemed to silently agree with her assessment. "Okay, you're probably right about the locals being too busy." Chris took her hand and led her outside. "But you need to stay close."

"Trust me, I will." The last thing she wanted was to be alone in the woods with Lanier on the loose.

Chris offered the scent bag to Teddy. The K-9 thrust his nose inside, then lifted it up in the air. The dog alerted near the front door of Skip's house, then continued circling the house.

Lexie liked to hike but keeping up with Chris and

Teddy as they went through the woods without the benefit of being on a trail wasn't as easy as she'd thought. Ignoring the ache in her knees, she pushed forward. No way was she giving Chris an excuse to send her back to the motel.

"Good boy," Chris praised, pulling a stuffed bear from his pack and tossing it up for the spaniel. Teddy plucked it out of the air and pranced around proudly. The dog had alerted in front of a boulder.

"Lanier must have rested here." She gazed around. "I wonder how long ago."

"That's the challenge," Chris admitted. "Teddy has a great nose, meaning he can find scents that may have been left several days ago."

"Meaning Lanier could have scoped this place out before he killed Skip."

"Yeah." He glanced down at Teddy. "I may need to call in some reinforcements from my K-9 team."

She could understand why he'd want extra hands or, in the case of their four-legged partners, feet on deck. This was a wide territory for one man and a dog to cover alone.

"Come, Teddy." The dog came over to sit beside him. Chris took the bear. "Seek! Seek Frank!"

Teddy whirled and continued making his way through the woods. Soon, though, it became clear they were going in a circle because she saw the roof of Skip's house.

Chris encouraged his partner to keep going, and the dog alerted halfway down Skip's driveway. The crime scene techs were already working on collecting evidence, so he didn't bother to head back inside. When he tried to continue, Teddy just looked up at Chris, as if asking, what more do you want?

"Lanier must have left his car here at some point," Chris said, crouching down to examine the ground more closely. "I don't see any tire tracks, though. Too many rocks. You might be right about Skip giving him a ride. It would explain why his truck isn't here."

She braced her hands on her hips, trying to breathe normally despite her exertion. "Now what?"

Chris was silent for a long moment. Then he rose and turned to face her. "We'll head back to the motel. I need to talk to my boss about these latest developments."

With a nod, she moved toward her Jeep. Chris took a few moments to take care of Teddy, giving him fresh water from the back of the SUV, before sliding behind the wheel.

She stayed close as they caravanned into town, hyperalert to their surroundings. She wouldn't put anything past Lanier, fully expecting him to jump out of the woods with a gun.

He didn't. Her phone rang, and she used the hands-free functionality to answer it. "Blue Skye Aviation, this is Lexie McDaniels."

"Oh, hi, you do the tours, right?" The woman sounded young, roughly her age.

"Yes, I do. Are you interested in flying over the Rockies?"

"I am," the woman gushed. "The only problem is that me and my husband are only here through tomorrow. Any chance we can go up in the morning?"

"I can do that, as long as the weather cooperates," Lexie said. "I won't take you up if there's a threat of storms in the area."

"Oh, I'm not worried. The forecast looks good," the woman said. "Thanks so much."

"I need your name," Lexie said. "And I'll want to run your credit card before we go up."

"Ashley Rauland. My husband is Derek Rauland and we'd like to pay in cash," she said. "I can be reached at this number if needed, but we'll be there in the morning."

"Okay, see you then." It wasn't the first time one of her customers wanted to pay in cash, but it wasn't that common, either.

She hoped Chris wouldn't be upset about her adding another tour at the last minute. She wasn't in a position to turn down paying customers.

Chris's SUV turned into the parking lot of their motel. She followed and parked next to him. He spent some extra time with his dog, so she used her key to access her room, sighing with relief at the air-conditioning.

Her knees throbbed so she gratefully sank down on the edge of the bed. All that walking had only added to her muscle aches.

"Are you okay?" Chris eyed her warily.

"Fine." She stared down at her scraped knees. "I look the way I did when I took my first skateboard ride." The moment she said the words, she wanted to call them back.

She never talked about her past, about her life growing up in New York City.

It was a slip she couldn't afford to repeat.

"Skateboard, huh?" The corners of his mouth lifted in a smile. "I did a lot of extreme sports when I was a kid, too. And I have the scars to prove it." He touched the deep groove over his eyebrow. "Drove my mom bonkers at the risks I'd take."

"Well, skateboarding was the extent of my extreme

sports," she said wryly. "I'm not as much of a daredevil as you must have been."

"I was that," he said with a grin. "Did you grow up here in Montana?"

She swallowed hard, finding it difficult to look into his eyes while lying. "In Helena, yes." She abruptly stood. "I'm going to take a shower if that's okay."

"Sure." Chris frowned as if he was taken aback by the change in subject. "Like I said, I have calls to make."

"Thanks." She edged past him and Teddy, disappearing in the bathroom.

She buried her face in her hands. Maybe she was just being overly paranoid about a possible connection between Lanier and her father. Yet if there was even the remote possibility that Lanier was coming after her because of her father's embezzling his money, she'd have to tell Chris the truth.

Soon.

Even if that meant losing him as a friend, forever.

Chris stared after Lexie for a long moment, before moving through the connecting door to enter his room. He pulled out his phone as Teddy curled up in the center of the bed.

Despite the fact that he still hadn't found Lanier, his partner had worked hard today. The dog deserved to rest.

"Russ? It's Chris Fuller. I need you to tell me everything you know about Skip Taylor. He was working as a mechanic for Blue Skye Aviation."

Russ clacked on the keyboard. "I did look up that name when Tyson filled in the team what's going on out there. Are you sure Skip is his real name? Usually, that's a nickname, sometimes for a man who might be a junior."

"A junior? Oh, you mean like named after his father." Chris pondered this. "I guess that could be right. Anyway, I think he was helping Lanier, only to be brutally murdered for his efforts."

"Things are heating up out there,"

"Tell me about it," Chris murmured. His failures were mounting so high, he began to doubt his ability to accomplish this mission. He needed to let his boss, Tyson Wilkes, know about how badly things were going.

Even if that meant Tyson's pulling him from the case and assigning someone else.

"I've been digging through several possibilities," Russ said. "Give me some time and I'll call you back."

"Thanks. Oh, and did you come up with anything on those four numbers?"

"No, sorry."

"That's okay." He knew the numbers were important, but four digits could mean just about anything. "Is Tyson around?"

"Not sure," Russ answered absently. "You want me to put you through to Jodie?"

"Yes, please." Chris's stomach churned as he waited for Tyson's assistant to pick up. "Hi, Jodie, can I speak to Tyson? I need to update him on the case."

"He's tied up at the moment, Chris." Jodie sounded upset. "There's been more trouble here at the training center."

He straightened and began to pace. "What kind of trouble?"

"Somehow the kennel was found unlocked and several dogs are missing," Jodie explained.

"Which ones?" Their K-9s were highly valuable animals, and he hated the idea of someone stealing them with the intent to sell them off to the highest bidder.

"Maverick and Angel," she said, indicating Reece Campbell's and Lucas Hudson's K-9 partners. "Along with three new recruits, Rebel, Shiloh and Chase."

Five dogs? "That's terrible, but how did the perp get to Maverick and Angel? Why weren't they with Reece and Lucas?"

"Reece and Lucas were both off-site on personal business and left the dogs behind," Jodie said with a sigh. "They're extremely upset, but not as much as Tyson. He knows he locked the kennel and is afraid this is just more proof someone has personally targeted RMKU."

"Yeah, I can see that." It was the only thing that made sense. First the incident during a training session with the dogs where a gun was shot off using a real bullet rather than a blank, and now this.

Was this an attack against the unit as a whole? Or was someone carrying a personal grudge against Tyson?

"I can ask Tyson to call you back," Jodie said, interrupting his thoughts. "Oh wait, here he is."

When his boss came on the line, Chris said, "Tyson? Are you okay?"

"We found Shiloh. Thankfully, as one of the newest dogs here, she didn't venture far from the kennels."

Chris closed his eyes for a moment, slipping into his old habit of silently thanking God for this blessing. The slip gave him pause. Maybe Lexie was right about God watching over them. "I'm glad to hear that."

"It's not good that someone has targeted the K-9s," Tyson continued. "I know I locked the kennel, so this was certainly no accident."

"I believe you," Chris assured him. "And I have no doubt you'll get to the bottom of it."

"Thanks for the vote of confidence." Tyson's tone was somber. "I'm sure we'll find the other four dogs and fast. Although I'm worried about Rebel. Our newest trainer, Tony Isaacs, thinks Rebel might be too head-strong to make a good K-9 and I fear he might be hard to find out there. If we do get him back, I'm not sure Rebel will make it through the program."

"Teddy had some trouble in the beginning of his training, but look at him now. He's a great K-9."

"Yeah," Tyson agreed. "I like Rebel, so I hope you're right. Now, enough about the issues here. What's going on with your case?"

He'd called in about the murder soon after finding Skip's body, but he hadn't gotten to speak directly to the sergeant. "I messed up badly," Chris confessed. He went on to explain about how he hadn't figured out that Skip was stalling, until it was almost too late. Then he stayed to board up the rear door of the hangar before heading out to confront the mechanic, only to find him lying on the floor in a pool of blood. "Skip's last dying words were to confirm that Lanier wanted Lexie and that he was sorry."

"I'm sure he was sorry for getting involved, but don't be so hard on yourself. Sounds like you saved Lexie's life, which is a good thing," Tyson said. "Did you give Russ any more details for digging into Skip's background?"

"I don't have much. He's working on that angle." Chris cleared his throat. "Look, Tyson, I totally understand if you want to send someone else here to take over. I know I should have Lanier in custody by now."

"You're the right man for the job, Chris." Tyson

spoke without hesitation. "You're a great, intuitive cop. And Teddy is one of our best trackers. I'm confident the two of you will find him."

His boss's support was humbling. "Thanks."

"I'll be in touch soon," Tyson said before disconnecting from the line.

Chris sat for a moment staring at his phone, thinking about the four missing dogs. It was a relief to know that Shiloh had been found, and he hoped the other K-9s would soon be located, too.

He said a silent prayer for their safety, a little surprised at how easily he'd returned to his faith, before getting up to pace again. So much was going on, back in Denver and here in Great Falls.

Unfortunately, he didn't have another lead to follow up on. Lanier had covered his tracks well. There was no doubt in his mind that the guy was holed up somewhere close by, waiting for the perfect opportunity to strike.

But where? And what kind of vehicle was he driving?

He debated calling Tyson back and requesting that Lexie be taken into protective custody. Not that she'd be willing to go along with that idea, but her safety was important to him.

What would Lanier do if he didn't have Lexie nearby to fly him out of there? Would he move on and find a new pilot?

He wants Lexie...

Skip's words echoed in his mind. He had no idea why Lexie was Lanier's target.

It was why he'd asked about where she'd grown up. She'd lived in Helena, so maybe Lanier had a previous interaction with her. Even something minor may have been enough for the guy to track her down here in Great Falls.

Was it his imagination or had she mentioned taking a shower just to avoid his questions? He turned and walked over to the connecting door between their rooms. She was still in the bathroom.

Telling himself to stop being paranoid, he was about to turn back when Teddy came over to stand beside him. Then his partner went all the way into her room, sniffing around as if looking for her.

"No, boy, here," he said in a low voice. He didn't want Lexie to think he was invading her privacy.

Teddy turned and looked at him. Since he wasn't wearing his vest, the dog knew he was off duty and therefore didn't jump to attention.

"You're more like Rebel than I thought," he said under his breath. He moved in and grabbed his collar. When he turned, he bumped into the table where her laptop computer was located.

The motion brought the screen to life. To his surprise, it wasn't password protected. He frowned when he saw the photograph of a man shaking another man's hand, smiling at the camera. The caption beneath the picture read: *Gerald and Ron Hall of Hall Investments support New York mayoral candidate Stephen Applegate at fun raising banquet.*

He stared at the photo, wondering why she'd pulled up this photograph on her computer. There must have been a reason.

Who were Gerald and Ron Hall, and why was Lexie interested in two men who lived on the other side of the country?

TEN

Lexie felt better after her shower, the hot water easing the soreness from her aching body. Physically, she'd heal fine, but emotionally?

She wasn't sure she'd ever cleanse the stench of Lanier from her senses, or forget his raspy voice telling her she was going to help him.

It all came down to the fact that he'd targeted her. She'd wracked her brain in an effort to remember if she'd ever seen Lanier with her father but had been unsuccessful. No doubt he'd seemed familiar, but she couldn't place him.

His comment about the money was perplexing, too. Upon escaping New York, she'd only taken the money she'd earned through honest work. She'd purposefully left her trust fund and her investments that had been tied with her father's and uncle's money behind.

No way had she wanted to touch any of the ill-gotten gains, she thought with a sigh. Especially since she'd made all those anonymous calls to the SEC to report her father.

Not that the information had resulted in any action against him. Every single time she performed a search on her father's name, she'd felt certain she'd read about his arrest and indictment.

But she hadn't. In fact, from the photograph of her father and Uncle Ron shaking hands with mayoral candidate Stephen Applegate, it seemed his arrest was highly unlikely.

When she emerged from the bathroom, she could hear voices coming from Chris's room. At first, she thought he was talking to Teddy, his K-9 partner, but then she realized he was on the phone.

"Thanks, Russ, get back to me as soon as possible," Chris said.

She waited for him to finish, hovering in the doorway between their rooms. When Chris saw her, a flash of guilt darkened his eyes. But then it was gone, as he tucked his phone in his pocket.

"Hey, you look great," he said with a smile. "I should probably shower, too, before we grab dinner."

"Okay." She tipped her head to the side. "What did your boss have to say about Skip?"

"Oh, that was actually Russ, our tech expert. He's the one searching for information on Skip."

"I still can't believe he's gone." She rubbed at her temple. "I wish I knew why he'd betrayed me."

"Hey, we'll figure it out." Chris's gaze was rather intense as he crossed over to take her hand. "Try not to think about it. You're alive, and that's what matters the most."

She offered a small smile. "I can't believe I'm saying this, but despite everything that's happened, I'm hungry."

He nodded and gently squeezed her hand. "Me, too. I'll be quick."

True to his word, Chris was ready fifteen minutes later. He took the time to feed Teddy before turning to her. "Would you rather eat in a restaurant or get some takeout?"

"Takeout." Maybe it was the impact of nearly being kidnapped by Lanier, but she wasn't in the mood to be surrounded by strangers.

"Okay, we've got Chinese or Italian." His topaz eyes twinkled. "Please choose Italian."

She laughed, something she hadn't done in what felt like forever. "Sure, Italian is great. Spaghetti and meatballs for me, please."

"A woman after my own heart." He used his phone to call in the order. "It'll be ready in twenty minutes."

She dropped into the chair at the small table. "How will uncovering the truth about Skip help us find Lanier?"

"You never know what can come up—a name from Skip's family or friends or previous coworkers that will connect to Lanier. A connection from anywhere that'll point to someone else who's involved. Leads come from the smallest details sometimes."

She nodded. "I hope your tech expert can find something."

He stared at her. "Is there anything else you want to tell me? Are you sure you don't know why Lanier has targeted you?"

She spread her hands. "I've done nothing but think about that over the past twenty-four hours. I can't come up with a single thing." *Unless Lanier is connected to my father, which seems impossible since he's here in Montana and not in New York.*

"What about when you were growing up in Helena?" Chris pressed. "Maybe your parents knew him."

"I don't think so." She hated lying to him and really, really didn't want to go down this path. "What about your parents?"

"Mine?" He looked shocked, then grimaced. "My mom passed away two years ago."

"Oh, Chris, I'm so sorry." She leaned over to rest her hand on his knee. "I shouldn't have pried into your personal life."

His smile was wan. "My mom was a Christian, just like you. She worked hard, holding two jobs when I was young to make ends meet. As soon as I was old enough to get a job, I did my part to help out."

Her heart ached for him. "I'm sure you did."

He covered her hand with his and met her gaze. "She was a great mom. But after she died, I found a letter she kept in a safe-deposit box, outlining the truth about my father."

She went still. "What truth?"

"That he was alive, for one thing," Chris said dryly. "Not dead the way she'd told me. And that they weren't married, like she also told me. They'd had a love affair, which produced me."

"Oh, Chris." She could only imagine how difficult it was for his mother to be pregnant without the benefit of a husband. She didn't know what to say to make him feel better.

"I'm not ashamed of that part," he assured her. "My mom found the church and believed in God, so I don't carry a grudge about the circumstances of my birth. She claimed she loved my dad, but that his family convinced him to leave her and to find someone within the rancher community." He lifted his gaze to hers. "So that's what he did. Leaving my mom to raise me all alone."

"That's terrible, for both of them," she said in a low voice.

"More for my mom," he said firmly. "My dad is now very wealthy. His marriage worked out for him. I also have a half brother, Ben Sawyer. He works in the K-9 unit with me."

"Wow, that's amazing. I'm glad you found your brother and your father."

Chris stood and looked away. "Yeah, well, I have a professional relationship with Ben. After all, he put in a good word for me with our boss, Tyson Wilkes. I doubt I'd be included on the RMKU team if not for Ben. But I have no plans to speak to my biological father, despite Ben's urging me to do that." He moved toward the door. "I'm heading out to pick up our food. Keep the door locked and bolt it when I leave. I won't be long."

"Okay," she said, but he'd already left the motel room, the door clicking shut behind him. She stood and shot the dead bolt home, then resumed her seat. Teddy looked up from his spot on the floor and gazed at her quizzically, before resting his head back down. She bent over to pet his soft brown-and-white fur. "He'll be back soon, Teddy."

Teddy thumped his tail in agreement.

She was surprised and thankful that Chris had chosen to share the details of his past with her. She sent up a silent prayer that God would help Chris find a way to forgive his father for the decisions he'd made in the past. Although she could understand that forgiving those who'd wronged you wasn't easy.

She and Chris had that much in common. He'd learned the truth about his father after his mother passed away. While she'd learned the truth about her father's illegal business dealings while her father was alive. Her father had also sent someone to kill her, which made her situation far worse.

Could she find a way to forgive her father? She closed her eyes and tried to find God's peace.

Fifteen minutes after he'd left, Chris knocked at the door. "Lexie? Open up."

She jumped up to unlock the door. He entered, bringing the enticing scent of oregano and tomato sauce with him. Her stomach growled.

Chris unpacked the food on the small table. When he sat beside her, she took his hand and bowed her head.

"Dear Lord, we thank You for this food we are about to eat. We also ask that You continue guiding us and keeping us safe from harm. Amen."

There was a slight pause before Chris echoed, "Amen."

"Thanks for participating." She took a small bite of her spaghetti and meatballs. "We need to have faith that God will continue to protect us."

He nodded. "I'll try, but I haven't been to church since learning of my mother's lies."

She inwardly winced. "Chris, if you think back to all the good times you had with your mom, the way she supported you, I think you'll find it easier to forgive her. She may have had a good reason to keep the truth from you."

He met her gaze. "I'll try, but my last girlfriend lied to me, too. In fact, I caught Debra cheating on me. As far as I'm concerned, there's never a reason to lie. It's something I really struggle with."

Her stomach knotted at his words.

No doubt Chris would be upset to learn about her secrets. Her lies. Born out of necessity to stay alive, but still lies.

Remembering their potent embrace, the sweetness of his kiss, made her realize that she needed to keep her distance from this point forward.

To protect her heart.

* * *

Chris wasn't sure why he'd told Lexie about his mom, and the truth about his father. Maybe he'd hoped she'd open up about her own past, since he knew nothing about her life before he met her, yet that hadn't happened.

She seemed focused on running her business, but hadn't she said something about knowing Skip for the past five years? What about before then? She hadn't talked about her life before moving to Great Falls, Montana.

Her prayer had touched him, though. Asking for God's support and guidance was something his mother would have done. And she had a point about forgiveness.

The idea of meeting his biological father was terrifying. More so because he wasn't sure he'd be able to hold his temper in check. Knowing his father was sitting in the lap of luxury while he and his mom had scraped by infuriated him.

Why hadn't the old man sent child support? And why hadn't his mother forced the issue?

He shook off the depressing thoughts and focused on his meal. The food was surprisingly good, especially since he hadn't eaten since breakfast.

"By the way, I have a tour tomorrow morning," Lexie said, interrupting the silence.

He shot her a quick glance. "I thought you didn't have anything scheduled?"

"A woman called while I was on my way here, asking for a tour for her and her husband before they head home."

He frowned. "I don't like it."

She arched a brow. "What's not to like? Her name

is Ashley Rauland. Her husband is Derek. I have her phone number if you want to check them out."

His scowl deepened. "It just seems odd that she called right after Skip was murdered."

She shook her head. "Look, I get you're a cop, Chris. But this woman is a tourist. How could she have learned about Skip or his murder so quickly? I'm not even sure it's hit the news yet. Besides, I'm not in a position to turn down a paying customer. If the weather cooperates, we're going."

He found himself hoping the weather wouldn't cooperate. A big storm blowing in from the mountains would be very helpful about now. Then a thought occurred to him. "What about the fact that you don't have a mechanic to check out the plane?"

She pursed her lips. "I'm sure the plane will be fine for one more flight, but you bring up a good point. I need to call Harry, to let him know we need to hire another mechanic, as soon as possible." She sighed, her expression turning grim. "Finding one in the middle of tourist season won't be easy."

He wanted to offer to help her locate one, but quickly stopped himself. He didn't know any plane mechanics, and really, this weird attraction he felt for Lexie was becoming a problem. Sure, she was beautiful, inside and out. Her kindness, her dedication to Skip despite how he'd turned against her was admirable.

But that's all he could allow himself to do, admire her from afar. No more holding her close and definitely no more kissing.

No matter how much he wanted to.

He reminded himself that he didn't do long-distance relationships. A woman as beautiful as Lexie likely didn't lack for male attention. Especially in Montana, where the men generally outnumbered the women.

Yet she hadn't mentioned a boyfriend.

Whatever. It didn't matter one way or the other. He wasn't in line for that particular role.

"That was delicious." Lexie set her fork down and sat back in her seat. "I'm stuffed."

"Glad you enjoyed it." He finished up the last of his pasta, too. "I need to take Teddy outside for a bit."

"I'll clean things up here," she offered.

Lexie's willingness to jump in and help out was sweet. Upon hearing his name, Teddy came over to nudge him, tail wagging with anticipation.

"I know it's time for you to go out." He put his K-9 on leash, since the dog wasn't wearing his vest. Sometimes Teddy could get a little rambunctious when it was playtime. He didn't mind, as Teddy was a great partner, but he wanted to be prepared. "Come, Teddy."

He glanced back at Lexie, who was smiling at Teddy. He told himself that Lexie's love for dogs wasn't enough to overcome the miles between them.

Debra had claimed to love dogs, too, but she'd insisted Teddy not be allowed up on the furniture. He'd tried to respect her wishes, but in hindsight realized things may not have ever worked out between them.

Even if she hadn't decided to cheat on him.

Chris shoved thoughts of Debra and Lexie aside to focus on Teddy. Since their arrival in Montana, they hadn't had much of an opportunity to play, which in the K-9 world meant practice. After Teddy took care of business, Chris put him through several drills, staying close enough to the motel so he could keep an eye on things. Teddy loved to play, and eagerly participated in whatever Chris asked of him.

He told himself he didn't need a woman in his life, not when he had a faithful companion in Teddy.

When they finished their play/training, he put Teddy back on leash and walked back to the motel. When his phone rang, he quickly answered. "Hey, Tyson, did you find the rest of the dogs yet?"

"Only one. Chase was located by Zara, Danielle Varga's Malinois," his boss informed him.

"I'm glad to hear it." Two of the five dogs had been found, and Chris wanted very much to believe the others would, too. "I'm surprised Maverick and Angel haven't returned. They're well trained."

"I'm concerned about that, too," Tyson admitted. "Makes me worry someone may have taken them." His boss paused, then added, "Or one of them is injured."

Either scenario was sobering. "Zara's good. She'll find them."

"I hope so." Tyson cleared his throat. "Russ is here. He wants to talk to you."

Russ was with the boss? That must mean their tech guru had found something significant. "Put him on. I could use a good lead because I've got nothing."

"Hold on, I'll put you on speaker." A second later, Tyson asked, "Can you hear us?"

"Loud and clear," Chris agreed. "Tell me what you know, Russ."

"I discovered that Skip's real name is Kipling Taylor the second," Russ said. "He shares the name with his father, Kipling Taylor the first."

"As we thought," Chris said. "But what about his background?"

"Well, that's the interesting part. Seems your dead guy spent time in jail for armed robbery."

It was interesting, but the timing didn't necessarily help his case. "He's been working here for at least five years, though, so he wouldn't have been in jail the same time Frank Lanier was. So how did Lanier convince him to turn on Lexie?"

"Seems that Skip had a bit of a gambling problem," Russ said. "It was part of the reason he'd ended up in jail ten years ago. He did five years, with time off for good behavior."

Gambling. Chris wondered if he should return to Skip's cabin to look for evidence of recent gambling. "So basically you're telling me that he owes people money and Lanier offered him cash as a way out."

"In looking through Kipling's bank records, he deposited one thousand dollars in cash two days ago. We believe that was his initial payment to help Lanier out."

A measly grand in exchange for Lexie's cooperation? Maybe even her life? The horrific thought sent him stumbling back a step. "That's not very much money, considering. And Skip should have known that Frank Lanier wouldn't hold up his end of the bargain." Then another thought occurred to him. "Wait a minute, where on earth did Lanier get a thousand dollars in the first place?"

"It's a good question," Tyson agreed. "We've always suspected Lanier had an accomplice. Maybe that person fronted Lanier the money."

"Yeah, maybe." They needed a lead on finding this mystery man, and soon. "Any ideas on who that is?"

"Negative," Tyson said.

Great. Chris scowled and ran his hand over his short hair. "Anything else?"

"Oh, yeah. You know that guy you asked me to look into?" The sound of paper rustling could be heard in the background. "Here, Gerald Hall, and his brother, Ronald Hall. They jointly own Hall Investments, although

Gerald had the company first and brought Ron in about seven years ago. They work as big-time financial advisers on Wall Street in New York."

"I saw a picture of them shaking hands with the mayoral candidate for New York City," Chris confirmed. "What do you know about them?"

"Nothing much, rumors about Hall being crooked, but no arrests on file. I dug up a family photo. Gerald has a wife, Abigail, a daughter, Savannah, and a son, Jeremy. Ronald's wife died a decade ago. I'll text the family pic over to you, just in case. You think there's some connection to Lanier?"

Lanier was convicted of killing a banker. Two of the men in the news article Lexie had open on her laptop screen were investment brokers. Again, why would she be interested in them? Had she made some connection between them and Lanier? Why, though? Who were the Halls and mayoral candidate to Lexie? "Just asking for personal reasons. Thanks."

Chris's phone pinged and he pulled it from his ear to look at the photo Russ sent.

There was a loud roaring in his ears, the pasta he'd eaten sinking heavily to the pit of his stomach. He stared in shock at a slightly younger version of Lexie standing between Abigail and Gerald Hall, along with her brother, Jeremy.

Her real name was Savannah Hall. She'd been lying to him, from the very beginning.

Just like his mother and Debra.

ELEVEN

After cleaning away the remains of their dinner, Lexie returned to her computer. She winced as she realized her father's photograph with her uncle Ron and the mayoral candidate was still up on her screen. She quickly closed that window.

She couldn't forget Lanier's comment about his share of the money. What share? Searching on Lanier, she found the article in the Helena newspaper about his conviction for murdering banker Brett Corea. She stared, her thoughts whirling.

If Chris was right about the possibility of the banker helping Lanier embezzle money, then she honestly didn't see how that could be connected to her father living in New York. There wouldn't be any reason for Gerald Hall to set up an embezzling scheme in Montana. Most of the big money was in New York or maybe Los Angeles. Even Chicago.

But Helena? Hard to imagine the capital city of Montana as being a target.

Unless her father knew she lived here?

As soon as that thought entered her mind, she dismissed it. If her father knew where she was, he'd have sent the same guy as before to kill her.

Lanier? Not likely, since the guy had escaped from a prison transport van.

She performed another search on her father, but instead of looking at the most recent photographs, she went back a good twelve months. Before the murder of banker Brett Corea.

Did she really think she'd find a picture of Lanier with her father? Maybe. She remembered the brief flash of familiarity upon seeing his mug shot.

A picture of her dad and her uncle Ron bloomed on the screen. She gasped when she looked closer. Her dad and her uncle were smiling at the camera, as usual, but it was a man standing off to the right who caught her attention.

Lanier.

The photo was grainy, and only showed Lanier's profile. Whom was he talking to? She couldn't tell. Was it really Lanier? Yes, the longer she looked at his face, his cheekbones and nose, the more she was convinced the guy was indeed Lanier. The escaped convict had been there. In New York, well over a year ago.

What did it mean? Could he have been one of her father's victims and lost money in a Ponzi scheme? That seemed likely now with the evidence in front of her.

She needed to show this to Chris.

The door to his room clicked open. Teddy came in first, followed by Chris. Glancing over at him, she frowned at his angry expression. Concerned, she jumped up. "What is it? What happened?"

"Why don't you tell me, *Savannah*?"

The name hit her with the blinding force of a sledgehammer. She stumbled backward, nearly tripping over her chair.

"What, you don't have anything to say?" His acid tone hurt worse than anything she'd experienced at Lanier's hands. "Why the lies, huh? What is it about certain women that they can't tell the truth?"

He'd uncovered her secret and hated her for it. After hearing about how his mother had lied, and how his girlfriend had, too, she could somewhat understand his reaction.

"I can explain," she said but he abruptly cut her off.

"Don't bother. I wouldn't trust a single excuse you have to offer. And the worst part is that I knew Lanier's attack on you was personal. I'm sure he's involved in your lies."

She managed to straighten her spine and lift her chin, refusing to cower over something she'd done to save herself. She gestured toward the computer screen. "You're right about one thing. I just found the proof that Lanier may be linked to my father."

His topaz gaze narrowed, as he darted a glance at the computer. "You expect me to believe you didn't know they were connected before now?"

She drew in a ragged breath. "I can't control what you believe, Chris. My father is a crook. In fact, I'm surprised he hasn't been arrested by now. I certainly made enough anonymous calls to the SEC. But look here, Lanier is in the background, so it makes sense that Lanier was one of my father's victims. I had no reason to connect them before now or think that Lanier could possibly know my real identity. I wondered, but I couldn't make sense of it until I saw this photo."

He moved closer, his gaze fixated on the laptop

screen. "That is Lanier," he admitted. "But if your father is an embezzler, why hasn't he been arrested?"

"I wish I knew." She swallowed hard. "He tried to—"

"Don't!" Chris harshly interrupted her. "I don't want to hear about your father, your family that you clearly left behind in New York. I only want to know why Lanier is fixated on you."

She wanted to explain about how her father had hired someone to break into her apartment five years ago, which was why she recreated herself, but he wasn't willing to listen.

"You already told me Lanier was part of the embezzlement scheme with Brett Corea, and that his DNA was found at the crime scene." She kept her voice even with an effort. "Maybe Corea hid some money, a fact that didn't come out at the trial. Now Lanier is trying to get the money and to get out of the state. He clearly found out who I really am. Using me could be his way of extracting revenge against my father."

"That scenario doesn't really work, *Savannah*. The facts don't line up. Like how did Lanier find you?"

The exaggerated emphasis on her former name hurt. She forced herself to face him. "My name is Lexie, and I don't know how Lanier found me." She was about to add that if Lanier found her, her father might know where she was—and why that was a big problem.

But Chris glared at her, then turned and disappeared through the connecting door before she could get out another word.

He closed his side, the lock sliding into place with a loud click.

Her knees went weak, and she sank down on the bed.

Her body felt hollow, as if a strong wind would break her into thousands of tiny pieces.

If she'd known about his mother's lie, or how his girlfriend had cheated on him, would she have told him the truth earlier? Probably not.

She buried her face in her hands, trying to hold back the sobs that wanted to erupt from deep within.

Looking back, she could see how she'd made a massive mistake. What if the tables had been turned and he was the one who'd lied to her? Reveling in Chris's embrace, enjoying his kisses and longing for more, without being honest with him, had been wrong.

No wonder he felt betrayed.

And the worst part of it all? He'd never forgive her.

Chris couldn't bear to look at Lexie. No, *Savannah*, he harshly corrected. Savannah Abigail Hall.

Once he'd managed to pull himself together, he'd gone in to confront her with the truth. Now all he wanted to do was to leave. Not just the motel, but Great Falls and this entire debacle of a case.

Only he couldn't do that. He might despise Lexie, a.k.a. Savannah, but he couldn't turn his back on the RMKU. Not after learning of the troubles his boss was already facing with the issues at the training center, including the missing dogs.

He paced the tiny room, trying to wrestle his emotions under some semblance of control. Unfortunately, Teddy picked up on his agitation, whining and weaving between his legs.

Forcing himself to stand still, he slowly exhaled. Bending over, he comforted Teddy.

"It's okay, boy. I'll be okay."

Teddy licked his hand.

His partner had successfully tracked Lanier, even if he was still at large. It wouldn't be fair to hand that task off to another team now. No, he would stay until he had Lanier in custody.

But he needed help, someone who could keep an eye on Lexie—*Savannah*—while he was working.

Ironically, the first person he scrolled through his phone to find was his half brother, Ben. It was nice to have someone he could count on for support.

Ben quickly answered. "Hey, Chris, are you okay? What's going on?"

Since he didn't normally call Ben with personal issues, his brother's question was understandable. "I've been better and could use some help," he confessed. "This case is growing more complicated by the minute."

"Happy to offer my assistance," Ben said without hesitation. "Hold on a minute, will you?" Chris heard a baby crying in the background, and mentally smacked himself for his rotten timing. Ben and his fiancée, Jamie London, had an infant daughter to care for.

He rubbed the back of his neck. This was hardly the time to ask Ben for help. Not when his brother had a woman and baby depending on him. One of the other RMKU officers could probably head over to offer assistance.

"I'm back," Ben said. "Barbara June is being a little fussy, but I'm telling you, Chris, she's the most beautiful baby in the whole world."

Chris was caught off guard by a surge of longing. Since the day he'd watched Debra cheating with another man, he'd told himself he didn't want or need a family.

So why the sudden urge to experience the joy and love that his brother had clearly found?

More proof his life was very different from his brother's. And not just because their father lived on a wealthy ranch.

Some things just weren't meant to be.

"I'm sure she is," he managed to respond through a voice hoarse with emotion. "I bet she's growing like a weed."

Ben let out a laugh. "So true. Now, you mentioned your case has sprung a few complications, so what is it that you need from me and Shadow?"

"Nothing, I don't want to take you away from Jamie and the baby. I'll find a way to deal with it."

"Hey, I want to help. Don't worry, Jamie will be fine. She's not here alone, she has plenty of support from our housekeeper, Mrs. E. Please, let me know what you need."

Chris was humbled by his brother's willingness to rush to Montana. It only made him realize that it was time for him to keep his promise to visit their father. The minute this case was over, he'd head to Wyoming to do just that.

"Chris?"

He pulled himself together. "Okay, here's the scoop. Lanier has made several attempts to kidnap Lexie Mc-Daniels. She's a pilot and owns her own plane. She works out of Blue Skye Aviation."

"Sounds as if Lanier wants to be flown somewhere safe," Ben commented.

"That's what I thought, but I believe he has a vehicle that he's using, so why not drive out of town to find another pilot to take him where he wants to go? Plus, there are plenty of pilots around the area. I recently learned that Lexie lied about her true identity. Her real name is Savannah Abigail Hall, and her father is some rich dude in New York City named Gerald Hall. It looks as if Lanier knows her father, so I think there's more to the story than what appears on the surface."

Ben whistled. "Wow, okay, so what can we do?"

"I'd like you to help watch over Lexie when she's at the Blue Skye Aviation hangar, while Teddy and I keep tracking Lanier."

"Are you asking me to do this because you're upset with her?" Ben asked.

He should have known his brother would read the truth between the lines. "You of all people understand why I can't stand to be lied to. First my mother, then my former girlfriend. It shouldn't be so difficult for people to tell the truth."

"Yes, I do understand how this may have impacted you," Ben agreed. "I know it's been hard for both of us over these past eighteen months to adjust to the truth about your mom, my mom and our father. I wish I could change how those events unfolded, but I can't. All we can do is to move forward from here."

"Yeah, right." He winced at the sarcasm in his tone.

"Chris, you know that God asks us to forgive those who trespass against us, and that includes your mother and our father." He paused and added, "Your ex and Lexie, too."

Easier said than done, Chris thought. Especially his mother's lies that spanned the course of his entire lifetime. Debra hadn't been the woman he'd thought she was. Lexie? He shied away from thinking about her. "Yeah, maybe. But right now, I need to stay focused on finding Lanier. If you're sure Jamie and Barbara June will be okay, I'd appreciate some help."

"I wouldn't leave them if I wasn't convinced they'd be fine," Ben countered.

"Thanks, I appreciate it."

"I'll get there as soon as possible," Ben assured him. "Oh, and, Chris?"

"Yeah?"

"Have you asked Lexie why she changed her name and moved halfway across the country?"

"No." She was about to explain, but he'd cut her off, unwilling to hear excuses.

"Sometimes there's a really good reason for keeping a secret." Ben paused, then added, "I'll give you a call when I get there."

"Thanks." Chris disconnected from the line, his brother's words echoing in his mind.

A good reason for keeping a secret? Forgiveness?

He grimaced and bent down to stroke Teddy's silky-soft fur. His brother was a better man than he was since Chris couldn't fathom such an insurmountable task.

He glanced back at the locked door between their connecting rooms. Feeling like an idiot for letting his anger get the better of him, he crossed over and unlocked and opened his side of the door.

Only to find her side was closed and locked, too.

Lifting his hand, he was about to knock, when he stopped himself. Maybe things were better this way. At least for now.

Turning away, he silently acknowledged he'd said things he shouldn't have. Maybe time apart would help him put what should have been a professional relationship with Lexie in perspective.

Just because they'd shared a few kisses didn't mean he had the right to act as if Lexie had cheated on him, the way Debra had. A lie wasn't the same as cheating.

Although it wasn't that different, either.

His phone rang. Recognizing Ben's number, he answered, "Did you change your mind about coming?"

"No, why would I?" Ben sounded exasperated. "I'm calling to let you know I have an early flight to Great Falls in the morning. Thankfully, Shadow doesn't mind flying, and I was able to rent an SUV, too. I should be at the hangar by eight or eight thirty in the morning. The flight time between Denver and Great Falls is only about ninety minutes."

"Okay, that works well. Despite hearing my concerns for her safety, Lexie has scheduled a tour that will leave at about ten, weather cooperating."

"I can understand why she needs to run her business," Ben said. "Does she know Shadow and I will be there with her?"

Chris glanced at the locked door between their rooms. "Not yet, but I'll fill her in."

"Might be helpful," Ben said dryly. "I don't want her to think I'm one of the bad guys."

"I know. I'll talk to her."

"See you in the morning, Chris."

"Yeah, see you then." He disconnected from the line and purposefully walked over to knock on Lexie's door.

A full minute ticked by before he heard the lock click. She opened the door and faced him, her eyes appearing red and slightly puffy. "What?"

Had she been crying? The urge to pull her into his arms was strong.

What was wrong with him? Lexie had betrayed him, yet he still wanted to comfort her.

"I—uh wanted you to know I've called in some reinforcements from the RMKU." At her blank look, he added, "The Rocky Mountain K-9 Unit headquartered in Denver."

"Okay." She didn't ask anything more.

"My brother Ben and his Doberman, Shadow, will be flying in early tomorrow morning. Shadow's expertise is in protection, so they'll be keeping an eye on you. They'll meet you at the hangar before your tour and hang out to wait for you to return."

She crossed her arms over her chest. "And where will you be? Heading back to Denver?"

"No, Teddy and I will continue searching for Lanier. I won't stop until we find and arrest him." He wanted her to know that despite their recent differences, he'd make sure to keep her safe from the man who had already killed three people.

This guy certainly wouldn't balk at killing more.

"Look where?"

He frowned. "I figured I should broaden our search area around the hangar. I should have found the dirt road back there sooner. Maybe there's something else we've missed." Even to his own ears, the plan sounded rather pathetic.

He really needed a lead. Learning that Lanier may know Lexie's father wasn't enough.

"I spoke to Harry, the owner of Blue Skye," Lexie said. "Local police had called him about Skip's murder. He's pretty upset."

The name reminded him that he hadn't interviewed the guy. "Where is Harry, again? I'd like to talk to him."

"Visiting his daughter and new grandson. He said he'd come back in a couple of days to deal with Skip's funeral."

If the owner of Blue Skye Aviation was actually out of town, he had a good alibi. "Give me his number, would you? I'd like to talk to him."

She nodded and grabbed her phone from the table. As she recited the information, he entered the numbers into his phone. "Have you met Harry's daughter?"

"Yes, she's about my age, and was married last year and recently welcomed a baby boy." Lexie frowned. "Why? You can't seriously believe Harry is a suspect in all of this."

He didn't point out that Skip ended up turning traitor, so why not Harry? "I just want to talk to him, that's all."

"Whatever." She crossed her arms over her chest again. "Anything else? Because I'd like to get some sleep."

"No, that's all I need." They stood awkwardly for a moment, the easy camaraderie between them gone, as if it had never existed. "Take care."

"Good night." She closed and locked the door.

He stared at the closed door, hating how much he felt as if he'd lost something precious.

Something he'd never get back.

TWELVE

Lexie didn't sleep well, her spinning thoughts constantly waking her up. Finally at five thirty she dragged herself out of bed and hit the shower.

Alone in her room, she made a cup of coffee and tried to settle herself. This edginess wasn't like her, and she needed to shake this off prior to her tour scheduled later that morning. A pilot needed to have a clear head before a flight.

Sipping her coffee, she found herself wishing she'd been given the opportunity to explain to Chris why she'd lied about her past. She'd had a good reason, but doubted the truth would make much of a difference.

From the very beginning, she'd known his aversion to secrets. She never should have dropped her guard around him. Never should have hugged and kissed him.

Knowing their relationship was ruined forever was what had kept waking her up. Her heart ached, far more than it should. For the first time in what seemed like eons until just today, she'd thought God had brought Chris into her life for more than just finding Lanier.

That maybe she didn't have to spend the rest of her life alone.

Selfish, really, as she should be grateful Chris had saved her life, more than once. And he'd assured her he'd stick around until Lanier was arrested.

Deep down, she knew Chris had called his brother in to avoid spending any more time alone with her. Sad, but true. The sooner she found a way to accept that their friendship was over, the better.

No matter how much it hurt.

With another K-9 cop *and* a Doberman to protect her, she felt more secure about her father likely knowing where she was. Telling Chris about all that—why she'd fled and changed her name—might sound like she was making excuses for not telling him who she really was.

After finishing her coffee, she opened her laptop and loaded her satellite software program to check the wind speeds and the overall weather conditions. Off in the distance, it appeared a storm may be brewing, but to her experienced eye, it looked to be several hours away.

Long enough for her to complete her tour before it hit.

She heard movement from the other side of the connecting door. Chris was up, likely taking care of Teddy. After a moment's hesitation, she stood and unlocked her side of the door.

Keeping the barrier between them seemed childish in the bright light of the morning. Chris's intent all along had been to keep her safe, while finding Lanier. Despite their kisses, the feelings she'd thought he'd expressed toward her had likely been a figment of her imagination.

His side of the door was still open about an inch. He must have heard her as he pulled it the rest of the way open. "Good morning."

"Morning." She did her best to sound normal. "I

wasn't sure if you were interested in getting breakfast. If not, I can head over to the restaurant alone."

"Breakfast sounds good," he agreed. "But I need to feed Teddy first."

"That's fine." The stilted conversation made her consider eating alone, regardless. Clearly, sharing a meal with Chris wouldn't be easy. "Let me know when you're ready."

"I will."

She returned to her room, blowing out a heavy sigh. Once his brother arrived, this forced togetherness would be over.

Chris took Teddy outside, returning about fifteen minutes later. Then he poked his head through the connecting door. "Ready?"

"Yes." She glanced around the motel room that had become a second home since Lanier had broken into her cabin. "Should I pack my things or leave them here?"

"Leave them. You can't go home until we have Lanier in custody."

She nodded and grabbed her purse, and they headed to his vehicle with Teddy in tow.

There were a few tables outside, and he gestured to them. "I don't think Lanier will try something when I'm sitting with you. Is it okay to eat out here?"

She suppressed the urge to look around for Lanier. "Sure."

They settled into seats across from each other, Teddy stretched out at Chris's feet. After they placed their order, Chris finally met her gaze. "I tried to get in touch with Harry Olson last night, but he didn't answer my call."

She frowned. "That's strange. Do you want me to try him?"

"That would be great." His gaze was serious over the

rim of his coffee cup. "I really need to verify where he spent the past few days."

"He's not involved in this," she protested, but pulled her phone from her small handbag. "I already told you he was staying with his daughter and grandson in Billings." She scrolled through her contact list and hit Harry's number. "A solid four-plus hours away from here. I don't think Harry was anywhere in the area while Lanier was on the loose."

"I'd still like to talk to him."

Chris didn't trust her judgment, and considering what Skip had done, she could hardly blame him.

Harry didn't answer her call, either, so she left a quick message. "Harry, it's Lexie. Give me a call when you have a minute okay? Thanks."

"You're sure you spoke to him yesterday?" Chris asked, his gaze slightly narrowed.

"Yes." Was he going to question everything she did from this moment on? "He was shocked to hear about Skip."

Chris didn't answer. Their server brought their meals. Lexie folded her hands in her lap and bowed her head to pray. She didn't reach for Chris's hand, the way she had in the past, but she did pray out loud.

"Dear Lord, we thank You for keeping us safe in Your loving arms. We ask you to continue guiding us on Your path, while teaching us to forgive others the way You sent Your only son to forgive our sins. Amen."

Chris didn't respond, but she hoped that maybe he'd think about the forgiveness part. His mother had taught him to believe in God, so maybe, just maybe those memories of attending church would return to the surface.

And if he chose not to forgive her? She tried not to wince, knowing there was nothing she could do to change his mind.

It was up to God to do that. Only God would be able to show Chris the way.

They ate in silence, the awkwardness stretching long between them. She tried to think of something to say, but Chris would barely look at her. When she couldn't stand it another moment, she set down her fork and tossed her napkin aside. "Excuse me."

He glanced sharply at her, as she stood and made her way inside the restaurant. She found the restroom, and stood at the sink, staring at her reflection.

This was more difficult than she anticipated.

Lexie reminded herself that she'd escaped New York, had relocated here in Great Falls to get away from her father, who wanted to kill her. This tenseness between her and Chris was nothing compared with what she'd gone through before.

Chris would be gone from her life, soon enough.

On her way back to the table, her phone rang. She relaxed when she recognized Harry's number. "Hey, I hope I didn't call you too early."

"No, I've been up. But what's the deal with this cop who called? What's going on down there?"

Chris glanced at her as she sat across from him. "Will you please talk to him, Harry? It's really important. Here, I'll give him the phone." She held the device out to Chris. "Harry's on the line."

"Mr. Olson? This is Officer Chris Fuller. Do you mind if I ask you a few questions?"

Lexie couldn't hear Harry's response, but he must have agreed because Chris continued. "Tell me exactly where you are." A pause, then, "Do you mind if I speak to your daughter?"

She picked up her fork and tried to eat, listening as Chris spoke to Harry's daughter, Amanda, and then to Harry again. His features relaxed to the point she figured he finally believed Harry was indeed in Billings, not someplace close by.

"Thanks, Mr. Olson. Here's Lexie." Chris handed her phone back.

"What in tarnation is going on?" Harry asked.

"Long story, but Skip has been murdered so you can understand why Officer Fuller wanted to verify your location. Just standard procedure, I'm sure." She did her best to soothe Harry's ruffled feathers.

"Murder?" Harry sounded surprised. She hadn't given him the details around Skip's death yesterday because she wasn't sure how much Chris would want her to say. "I thought he had a heart attack or something. Maybe I should come back today, talk to the police in person."

"No rush—well, other than we need to find another mechanic to help out." Skip's pale features flashed in her mind. No matter what Skip may have done, he didn't deserve to die. "I have a tour today, but nothing scheduled for tomorrow."

"I'll get on that," Harry agreed. "And I'll call you when I get back to Great Falls."

"Thanks, Harry." She ended the call and tucked the phone back in her purse. Meeting Chris's gaze, she added, "I hope that helped put your mind at ease."

"It does." Chris finished his meal and pushed his plate aside. "I used my map program to verify that his daughter does live in Billings. I'll ask Russ to trace the call, just to be sure they're both there."

She nodded, wondering what it was like to go through life suspecting everyone of being a crook, until proven otherwise.

Similar in many ways to what she'd experienced back in New York.

The only difference was that she preferred to think of people as innocent until being proven guilty.

Not the other way around.

Sitting across from Lexie was pure torture.

Despite his best efforts, Chris couldn't seem to keep his emotions from running amuck. He'd eaten his breakfast in record time, anxious to get this meal over with.

Ben and Shadow couldn't get here soon enough.

Talking to Harry didn't exactly prove he was in Billings, and he'd been forced to leave a message for Russ to trace the call. Chris didn't want to think his daughter would lie for him. Then again, why wouldn't she?

Don't go there, he warned himself. Even he knew that distrusting everyone about everything wasn't healthy.

Lexie's prayer about forgiveness had hit hard. It was the same advice Ben had given him. Chris knew he needed to get over it already.

He should stay focused on Lanier. Glancing at his watch, he realized they still had a full hour before Ben would arrive.

As if reading his mind, Lexie broke the silence. "If you want to head out to track Lanier, I can grab a rideshare to the hangar later."

Her offer was tempting, but he shook his head. No point in being a coward. "I'll wait until Ben arrives."

"Okay."

Teddy shifted at his feet. An idea hit him. "Where does Harry live?"

Lexie eyed him suspiciously. "Why? You don't believe he's visiting his daughter?"

"I do," he hastily assured her. "But it could be that Lanier stumbled across Harry's home at some point. With Harry out of town, it would be beneficial to check it out. We have time," he added. "We can swing by on our way to the hangar."

"If that's what you want to do," she reluctantly agreed. "His place isn't that far from the hangar, closer to me than to Skip."

He wanted to kick himself for not thinking of this sooner. Especially after what had happened to Skip. Glancing at Lexie's plate, he forced himself to wait for her to finish the last few bites of her omelet. He paid the bill as she finished.

"I'm ready." She set her napkin aside and rose to her feet.

"Come, Teddy." He kept his partner on leash as they walked the short distance back to the motel. There, he took a moment to put Teddy's working vest on and grab his backpack before loading the dog in the SUV. He frowned when Lexie headed toward her Jeep. "I thought we'd drive together."

"Really?" She glanced back at him. "I would have thought you'd prefer to drive alone."

"I'll drive you," he said firmly. "Better that we stick together, especially if we're stopping at Harry's first."

She didn't answer but came over to get into the passenger seat.

"I'm sorry," he said, once they were seated. "I know I came down hard on you. I'm sure you had your reasons for leaving New York and setting up a business here under a fake name."

"I did have a reason." She didn't elaborate. "And I'm

sorry I lied to you. But I honestly never imagined the possibility that Lanier knew my father. Or at least, was at the same function my father attended."

"You mentioned your father was a crook."

"Yes." She stared through the windshield. "I stumbled across proof that his business was corrupt and confronted him. That conversation didn't go well, so I left." She shifted a bit in her seat. "I've made anonymous calls to the SEC over the years, but as you could see, my father hasn't been arrested for his crimes."

The idea that Lanier may have been one of her father's victims was an interesting angle. Yet he couldn't seem to make the puzzle pieces fit together. Maybe Lexie hadn't told him *everything*.

"Turn right at the next intersection," Lexie instructed. "Harry's place is on the left."

He followed her directions, nearly missing the opening to Harry's driveway. These houses that were practically buried in the wilderness were very different from the area where he lived in Denver.

He thought of Lexie's remote cabin. How did she manage to live so far away from other people? Or maybe she'd purposefully chosen the location because it *was* far away from others.

Harry's house soon came into view. The place certainly appeared deserted, no vehicle or people in sight. Although that's how Skip's place had looked before they'd found the mechanic lying in a pool of blood on the floor after being attacked by Lanier.

His gut tightened as he carefully swept his gaze over the area. Harry's house was larger than Lexie's and Skip's, almost double in size. Where had Harry gotten his money? Enough money to pay for a large house, a hangar along with several acres of land, two planes and a

vehicle. Was it possible Harry was involved in the embezzlement scheme that had resulted in the banker's death?

At this point, nothing would surprise him.

"Wait here," he said to Lexie, as he pushed open his
door. Thankfully, she didn't argue.

He let Teddy out of the back, shouldered his pack and
pulled his weapon. He cautiously made his way toward
the front of Harry's house. Peering in through the window, he didn't see anything amiss. After methodically
making his way around the entire structure, looking
into every single window, he was forced to admit Lanier
wasn't hiding out here. Harry wasn't there, either.

Because he was truly innocent? Or because he'd set
the wheels of Lanier's escape in motion and then high-
tailed out of town so he'd have an alibi?

He glanced at his watch. There was still time to do
a quick search for Lanier on the property. He offered
the scent bag to Teddy, who eagerly sniffed at the scrap
of fabric inside.

"Seek! Seek Frank!"

His K-9 went to work lifting his nose and then taking off on some invisible scent path that only Teddy's
keen nose could pick up.

It didn't take long for Teddy to alert near the back
door of Harry's home. The hairs on the back of Chris's
neck rose in alarm.

Lanier had been here. But when? Recently? Or days
ago?

"Good boy," he praised. "Seek Frank!"

Teddy gamely put his nose back to the ground and
headed off in a path that wound around the other side
of the house to a flat area behind a trio of trees. Teddy
alerted there, and when Chris saw the familiar boot

print in the ground, he pulled the bear from his pocket and tossed it to the dog.

"Good boy!" He looked around, wondering if Lanier had walked this way after escaping Lexie's house the night he'd attacked her. The map in his head indicated Lexie's house was about a mile from here.

He decided to go just a little farther. After gently taking the bear, he offered the scent bag again. "Seek Frank."

The dog whirled and once again picked up the scent. He holstered his gun, since the dog was taking him deeper into the woods.

After about fifty yards, Teddy alerted again. This time, Chris could see the tire marks in the soft earth. Using his phone, he snapped several pictures and sent them off to Russ with the request to see if there was enough tread to identify a make and model of the vehicle Lanier was using.

"Good boy," he praised his partner.

Teddy wagged his tail and nudged the pocket where he kept the bear.

He gave the dog his reward. As he turned to retrace his steps back to where he'd left Lexie, his phone buzzed.

"Russ, do you have something?"

"I wanted you to know I was able to verify that phone number you asked me to trace did come from Helena. Boss also wanted me to let you know all the missing dogs have been found, although he's still pretty steamed about the whole incident. Regarding the tire tracks, all I can tell you is that the tires could be for a pickup truck. So far, I haven't been able to narrow down anything more specific."

Lanier potentially using a pickup truck was more

than he knew before. The news about the missing dogs, was a relief, yet the attacks against the team itself was a serious concern. Something he'd need to follow up on, later. "Thanks, that's helpful."

"Oh, and I have one more thing." Chris could hear paper rustling in the background. "I was able to lift a partial index finger from that scrap of paper with the four numbers on it."

"You were? Tell me they were a match to Kipling Taylor or Lanier."

"No, that's the surprising part," Russ said. "I got absolutely no hits off the partial print in the AFIS database."

Chris frowned as he pushed through the woods. "That doesn't make any sense. Both Lanier and Taylor have criminal records. Their prints are in the system."

"I know." Russ's tone turned grim. "I'm afraid there could be someone else involved. Someone whose prints aren't on file."

"Yeah," Chris agreed slowly. "Thanks."

"If I find something more on those tire treads, I'll let you know." Russ disconnected from the call.

Chris reached Harry's driveway with Teddy, still trying to understand the implication of the partial print.

Teddy had alerted on the scrap of paper that Chris had plucked out of the garbage at the hangar, so that meant Lanier must have had it at some point.

Who was the mystery person, and how did he or she factor into the case?

THIRTEEN

Lexie was relieved to see Chris and Teddy emerge from the woods. She could tell Teddy had alerted at some point, because of the way he'd lifted his nose in the air and gamely plowed through the brush.

It seemed as if Frank may have been there recently. She'd defended Harry Olson, but deep down had been worried because she didn't know Harry any better than she knew Skip.

Maybe Chris was right about secrets.

His previous anger had faded, and she was glad his attitude toward her had been professional that morning. She missed their closeness yet had no one to blame but herself.

Chris opened the back hatch. Teddy gracefully jumped inside. When Chris slid behind the wheel, he glanced at her. "Teddy found Frank's scent, but the trail ended at the dirt road, where I found some tire tracks. Likely belonging to the truck we believe Lanier is using."

"I assumed Teddy found something, the way you both disappeared into the woods."

Chris started the SUV and began backing down the driveway. "Does Harry have a criminal record?"

"Harry?" She was shocked by the question. "Not that I'm aware of, why?"

"Did you know Skip's real name is Kipling Taylor and that he had a criminal record? He spent five years in jail."

The blood drained from her face. "No! For what? What did he do?"

"Armed robbery." Chris's tone was matter-of-fact. "After I drop you at the hangar, I plan to dig into Harry's past, make sure he doesn't have a criminal background, too."

She slowly shook her head. "It's as if I've been living in a bubble. How is it possible Skip spent time in prison?"

"His gambling debts got out of control."

Gambling. Maybe she didn't know the real Skip or the real Harry.

Then again, neither of the two men knew the truth about her identity. *Secrets.* She couldn't suppress a shiver.

The drive to the hangar didn't take long. She glanced at Chris's handsome profile several times, wishing that things could be different.

That he didn't feel as betrayed by her secrets as he'd been by his mother.

There were no other cars in the parking lot when they arrived. Without Skip and Harry, the place was desolate. Oh, there was plenty of activity several miles away at the main airport terminal, but here in the rather isolated area where Blue Skye's private hangar was located? Not so much.

Lexie found herself wondering if she'd be able to

keep her business afloat for the long term. Great Falls, Montana, had been her refuge over these past five years.

Her sanctuary.

But now? Chris knew the truth, and maybe Lanier did, too. She just couldn't be sure. Maybe Lanier had another reason for thinking she knew something about "his money." Something connected to her as a local pilot and her plane. But if Lanier did know who she really was, others might learn about her identity, spreading the word all the way back to New York. If that happened, she'd have to pack up, change her identity and start all over again.

A truly depressing thought.

"Stay here while Teddy and I check the place out and keep the doors locked," Chris said. "Could I have your keys?"

"Don't you want to wait for your brother?"

"No need, I'm capable of doing a sweep of the area."

She sighed and dropped the keys into his outstretched palm. "Be safe, Chris."

A flash of surprise darkened his topaz eyes before he gave a curt nod. "We will."

Lexie sent up a silent prayer asking God to watch over Chris and Teddy as they set out to explore the area. A few minutes into their task, another SUV pulled up next to her. She smiled at the handsome man behind the wheel. Chris's brother. Ben looked different from Chris, yet they were both tall and shared the same topaz eyes and the dimple in their chin. Chris had mentioned they had different mothers, but she doubted Chris would confide more personal details about his parents to her.

Maybe once, before she'd ruined everything, but not any longer.

Ben let a tall Doberman out of the back of his SUV, then came over to open her door. "You must be Lexie."

"Yes, Lexie McDaniels." She felt guilty for using her new name, even though she had legally changed it. "And you're Ben, right? It's nice to meet you."

"Yes, I'm Chris's younger brother." Ben shook her hand, then glanced down at his dog, a black Doberman pinscher with cinnamon markings on his face. He was large and looked extremely capable of his duty to protect. "And this is Shadow."

"Very nice to meet you, too, Shadow."

"Where's Chris?" Ben turned to scan the area. "Oh, I see him. Stay here, Lexie, with the doors locked. We'll let you know when it's safe to come out."

"Okay." She closed the door and watched as the two brothers greeted each other before continuing to clear the area. Less than five minutes later, Ben returned. "All set, Lexie."

"Thanks." She joined the officers inside the hangar. "I'm going to check the weather again, then pull the plane out. I'm not a mechanic, but thankfully I have learned a few things from Skip over the years." Thinking of Skip as an armed robber, doing jail time, made her sad.

"I'm sorry to hear about Skip's murder," Ben said. "I'm sure that was a terrible shock."

"It was." Almost as much as finding out that she didn't know much about the man who'd kept her plane and Harry's in tip-top shape.

"Lexie, do you mind if I borrow your office computer?" Chris asked. "I need to check something."

"Of course, help yourself." She followed the two officers and their K-9 partners to her small cubicle area.

She entered her password, then stepped back so Chris could take over the keyboard.

It was frighteningly easy for Chris to access the information he needed. She found herself breathing a sigh of relief when he finished. "Looks like Harry is clean."

"That's good," she said. But when Ben and Chris exchanged a knowing glance, she frowned. "Isn't it?"

"Yeah, it's fine." Chris moved out of the way and turned toward his brother. "I'm going to take Teddy out to walk along the dirt road again. You'll stick around the hangar?"

"Yep."

"Thanks. Come, Teddy." Chris led the K-9 out of the small office and disappeared outside.

"Sorry you've been stuck with babysitting duty," she said.

"Protective detail," Ben corrected with a grin. "And I don't mind backing up my brother. I was honored he'd asked."

She nodded and took a few minutes to verify the weather conditions. A storm was still lingering over the mountains, but based on the wind, she didn't think it was close enough to cause alarm. The weather could be unpredictable, but she felt certain she'd have her tour group back on the ground before the storm hit.

"I'm going to walk the perimeter of the hangar with Shadow," Ben said. "I want Shadow to know the area, but I plan to be back before the couple shows up for their tour. What time do you expect them to arrive?"

She glanced at her watch. It was quarter to nine, and she figured her guests may come early. "Probably in an hour or so."

"Okay, stay inside the hangar for a bit. We'll be back soon."

She nodded, then turned back to her computer. She did another search for her father but didn't find any new pictures of him on social media.

Because he was busy? Or because he'd hopped a plan to Montana?

She'd gone back and forth about Lanier connecting her to her father but couldn't be sure. As she'd considered when she'd first seen the photo of her dad, uncle and the mayoral candidate with Lanier in profile, if her father knew where she was, he'd have sent someone to kill her by now. And not Lanier, who'd been on his way to prison before he'd escaped the prison van. So maybe Lanier was after her for another reason.

No, she honestly didn't think her father knew where she was or that he'd come after her himself. He'd definitely send someone else to do his dirty work. Just like he had hired someone to follow and break into her apartment back in New York.

Frank Lanier? Maybe. Now that she thought about it, Frank could have been the one to have done that five years ago. But it didn't make sense that her father would have hired him again, now mere days after he'd escaped from a prison van ninety miles from here. How would her father have gotten in contact with Lanier?

Not entirely reassuring to consider the possibility someone else may be after her.

Lexie told herself not to borrow more trouble; she had plenty to worry about with Lanier on the loose.

She finished tidying up her workspace, then checked the satellite one more time, before heading over to her

Cessna. Her bird was tucked near Harry's Cessna, where Skip had left it.

With a sigh, she opened the hatch over the engine and peered inside. She only knew enough to get by, and once she was satisfied that things looked good, she closed the panel.

Dragging the Cessna outside wasn't difficult. She released the tripod rolling brackets and slid them back out of the way. Remembering how Ben had told her to stay inside, she winced and climbed into the cockpit.

She heard footsteps, and figured Ben had returned. Only the same awful stench she'd come to associate with Frank Lanier wafted toward her. She opened her mouth to scream, only to suck in a harsh breath when she saw the barrel of a gun inches from her face.

"If you scream, I'll shoot you somewhere nonlethal," Frank said. His eyes were cold as ice, his face scruffy and his clothes wrinkled and sweat stained, as if he really had been living in his car over the past few days. "There's no one to hear you, anyway."

No one? The ice congealed in her stomach. "What did you do to Ben and Shadow?"

"They are not your concern. Getting me out of here is. Understand?"

She nodded, subtly trying to find where Ben and Shadow were. Chris and Teddy, too. "Did you arrange the tour?"

"Yeah, I paid some woman to do that for me." Frank opened the rear door and jumped in behind her before she could move. His threat to shoot her someplace that would only hurt, rather than incapacitate her, wasn't an idle threat. He needed her alive because he wanted something from her. Then he'd kill her. This man had already murdered at least three people, likely more.

"Close your door." Frank's raspy voice made her shiver. His body odor was so bad, it was all she could do not to vomit.

She closed the door, then didn't move. Deep down, she wanted to stall for as long as possible. Once they were in the air, it would be too late. But while they were on the ground, there was a small chance of being rescued.

Maybe Ben and Shadow weren't hurt very badly. Maybe Chris and Teddy were already making their way back to the hangar.

Maybe... The thought abruptly cut off as Frank shoved the barrel of the gun against the back of her neck. "You're going to do exactly as I say, understand?"

"Yes." Her voice was barely a whisper.

She stared out at the blue sky. *Please, Lord, keep me, Chris, Ben and their K-9 partners safe from harm!*

Chris and Teddy had scoured the area behind the hangar without finding anything significant. A nagging feeling wouldn't leave him alone.

He was missing something, a very large piece to the puzzle. But what?

The mysterious partial fingerprint on the scrap of paper he'd found beneath Skip's workbench bothered him. He'd been wracking his brain to come up with who might be Lanier's accomplice.

Harry hadn't been here recently but discovering the owner of the hangar didn't have a criminal record moved him back to the suspect list. The prints they'd found on the slip of paper were from someone without a criminal record. Most likely someone familiar with the area. Harry could have easily helped Lanier escape, even providing the convict a vehicle, before heading out to hide at his daughter's house. With transportation and money, Lanier could have done the rest on his own.

But it all came back to motive. Why would Harry help Lanier escape? Money? The guy didn't seem to be doing very badly. In addition to looking up Harry's criminal record, he hadn't found any evidence of debt within the circuit court system.

Then again, some people weren't satisfied with what they had. They always wanted more.

Harry Olson may have wanted more money. Chris wondered how much cash Lanier may have taken after killing the Helena banker Brett Corea but before he was arrested and thrown in jail. Enough to justify killing the deputy and Skip in order to retrieve it?

And the biggest question of all was why Lanier was so focused on Lexie.

His anger toward Lexie had faded to the point he'd regretted dragging Ben and Shadow away from Jamie and her daughter. Leaving Lexie to his brother made sense, because Shadow was trained as a protector while Teddy was trained to track down the bad guys.

But he couldn't deny the itchy feeling crawling along the back of his neck. He trusted Ben. His younger brother had been an army ranger and could easily take care of himself.

So why was his gut telling him to rush back to the hangar to check on Ben and Lexie? Glancing at his watch, he realized her tour should be showing up any minute.

Unable to stop himself, Chris called Teddy to come.

Then he broke into a jog, taking the shortest distance between the dirt road and the hangar parking lot.

As he burst through the trees, he narrowed his gaze when he saw a battered truck parked off to the side. Lexie's tour? No, it was Skip's truck.

But Skip was dead.

Pulling his weapon from his holster, he edged forward, raking his gaze back and forth.

Where were Ben and Shadow? They should have noticed him approaching by now.

He crossed the parking lot, coming to an abrupt stop when he saw his brother and Shadow lying on the ground.

"Ben!" His shout erupted from his throat. He dropped beside his brother, stunned to see a dart imbedded in his brother's thigh. He ripped it out, then saw another dart was imbedded in Shadow's flank, beneath his vest, and removed that one, too.

His brother was breathing, and so was Shadow, but he quickly called 911 requesting an ambulance. What drug had been used on them? A sedative, maybe even a narcotic? Rummaging in his pack, he found the two doses of Narcan, a medication used to counteract narcotics that they always carried with them.

If the drug used wasn't a narcotic, the dose wouldn't hurt either of them. He squirted one dose into Ben's nose, and the other dose into Shadow's mouth. His brother groaned and blinked. "Chris?"

"You're okay, and so is Shadow. The ambulance is on the way. Where's Lexie?"

Ben's brow furrowed. Then Chris heard the sound of a plane engine.

No! Lexie!

He didn't want to leave his brother and Shadow behind, but when he saw the plane wheeling out of the hangar, a man's profile behind Lexie sent a chill down his spine.

The tour setup was a trap! Lanier was on the plane with Lexie.

"Go," Ben urged weakly. "Hurry!"

Chris didn't give himself a chance to change his mind. He rose and bolted after the plane, Teddy keeping pace as he ran. At some level, he wanted the dog to stay back where it was safe. Only the two of them were a team.

Always together, no matter what.

The plane was gathering speed. He didn't bother trying to call out to get Lexie's attention. She wouldn't be able to hear him over the loud plane engines.

He pushed himself harder, Teddy still at his side. If the dog couldn't make it, he prayed Ben would watch over his partner.

No matter what, Ben would be there for him.

There was no time to regret the mistakes he'd made regarding his brother. He focused on gaining ground on the plane, sending up a silent prayer that he would be strong enough, fast enough to grab hold.

Two feet, one foot, six inches. *Got it!*

He grabbed the door handle and wrenched it open. Teddy was still beside him, so he reached down, grabbed the K-9's vest and tossed him inside, before hauling himself into the plane.

Lungs heaving, he struggled to find his voice, shouting over the din of the twin engines. "Stop the plane, Lexie! Frank, there's no way to escape. I'm here to arrest you and to haul you back to jail."

"I don't think so." The escaped convict smiled humorlessly. It took Chris a moment to realize the guy had a gun pressed into the back of Lexie's neck.

He belatedly realized that this was the reason Lanier hadn't tried to shoot him to prevent him from climbing into the plane. Because he couldn't risk moving the gun or his leverage long enough for Lexie to knock the gun out of his hand.

And there wasn't anything Chris could do to change it.

Frustrated, he grabbed the closest headphones, so that he could communicate with the two of them. He tried to calm his racing heart. He needed to come up with an escape plan.

"I rescued my brother and his K-9," he said into the headset. "They're going to be fine, despite you shooting them with tranquilizer darts."

Lexie gasped, but Lanier simply shrugged. "Too bad, the world would be a much better place with one less cop and nosy dog on the streets."

"You won't get away with this," Chris threatened.

Lanier pushed the gun muzzle firmly into the back of Lexie's head. "Get us off the ground, now!"

She didn't argue. The plane accelerated, then lifted up and off the ground, heading into the clear blue sky. Chris swallowed hard as he watched the ground disappear beneath them.

There had to be a way out of this mess. There just had to be!

Ben would call for backup, maybe even find a way to get his hands on another plane to come rescue them. But he didn't have high hopes that anyone would be able to find them quickly enough.

"Where are we going?" he asked.

There was no response from Lanier.

"I need to know our destination, Frank," Lexie added calmly. "I can't just fly in circles, especially since you didn't give me time to complete a thorough plane inspection before taking off."

"I'll give you the coordinates," Lanier said. "Pay attention, your life depends on it. You're going to head 45.8342 degrees north and 111.8628 degrees west. Got it?"

"Yes, I understand," Lexie said. "But why do you want to go to the Lewis and Clark Caverns?"

The numbers 111.8 were echoing in Chris's mind. He'd never thought about a GPS coordinate. If he'd mentioned the scrap of paper with the numbers on it to Lexie, she likely would have known right away what they meant.

His keeping the evidence a secret may very well result in their deaths.

FOURTEEN

Despite the cold hard metal gun barrel shoved against her nape, Lexie strove to remain calm. Panic wouldn't help her right now, not if there was the possibility of getting out of this alive. She wanted to look at Chris, ask why he'd come jumping onto the plane, but didn't dare move her head for fear of catching Lanier off guard.

She didn't trust the guy not to kill her by mistake.

Her emotions were a massive knot in her belly over Chris's presence in the bird. It felt good not to be stuck alone with Lanier, yet she feared Chris's heroic and acrobatic act of getting up and into the plane would only result in his death, and Teddy's, too.

Please, Lord, please spare our lives!

She banked the plane in a gentle curve around the mountain, trying to come up with a plan that wouldn't result in the three of them being killed while Lanier got away scot-free. There had to be something she could do. Did she risk landing at the caverns as he'd ordered?

What if Lanier took that opportunity to kill Chris and Teddy, getting them both out of the way? Once they reached the Lewis and Clark Caverns to get whatever money he was looking for, Lanier must have a plan for her to fly him to another location, someplace far away.

No doubt that was when he planned to kill her, escaping for good.

"How long will it take to get to the caves?" Lanier asked.

She didn't immediately answer.

"Savannah," he hissed. "How long?"

Stunned by the use of her real name, she tightened her grip on the stick. "How did you find me?"

"How long?" His voice was so loud in her headset, she winced.

"Thirty minutes, give or take a few," she answered, untruthfully. "Why do you want to go there, anyway?"

"I told you, I want the money."

What money? She wanted to scream at the top of her lungs but managed to maintain control. If she lost it at this altitude, they would all die.

An icy-cold finger of fear slid down her spine. No, that was not an option.

She blew out a breath and focused on coming up with a plan. It had been a long time since she'd flown to the Lewis and Clark Caverns. If her memory was correct, there was a strip of grass that could be used as a runway. It wasn't optimal, but better than nothing.

Which made her wonder why Lanier wanted to come here. Had Brett Corea hidden money in the caverns? Or Lanier himself? Maybe Harry had taken one of them to the caves, before Lanier had murdered Corea and gotten himself arrested.

Yet she couldn't help but think that there was something more going on. Lanier had called her Savannah. He'd purposefully found her at the hangar.

Maybe he *had* been sent by her father.

A sudden chill hit hard. Was it possible her father had known where she was hiding all along? Did he have someone within the SEC on his payroll? Had her multiple calls to the SEC requesting an investigation into her father's criminal activities given her current location away?

The idea was sobering.

"My brother is going to send a plane out to find us." Chris's voice was calm through her headset. "You're not going to get away with this."

"Maybe, but it won't matter. There are many places to fly amid these mountains. And they won't know our final destination, will they?" Lanier gloated. Then his voice hardened. "Fly faster, Savannah," he ordered. "And if you see another plane, ditch them."

Lexie felt certain that they'd be at the caverns long before another plane had a chance to rescue them. Especially as she'd lied about how long it would take to get to there. The well-known caves were getting close now, and if Lanier was able to read her instrument panel over her shoulder, including the dials displaying their current latitude and longitude, he'd find that out soon enough.

She dropped the plane's altitude to prepare for landing. Yet she worried that the minute they were on the ground, Lanier would start shooting.

Was a rescue plane really on the way? Should she take another circle above the caves, hoping Lanier wouldn't notice?

No, she quickly dismissed that idea. Being held at gunpoint would make a successful rescue by another plane pretty much impossible. Lanier had Chris and Teddy as hostages, too. If Lanier shot her, they would all die, but that wouldn't prevent Lanier from turning his weapon against Chris or Teddy.

The horrible thought gave her an idea. She saw the stretch of grass that would work as a pseudo landing strip and dropped her altitude a bit more.

"What are you doing?" Lanier asked. "Get us back in the air."

Since he hadn't noticed the caverns below, she ignored him. Instead, she abruptly jerked the stick side to side. Waving her wings back and forth sent the plane rocking with enough force to knock Lanier off-balance.

"Stop that!" Lanier's tone was panicked. "Stop!"

He moved the weapon away from her neck for several long moments. Was it enough? Yes! She heard Lanier's muffled grunt as Chris attacked him, struggling for the weapon.

Now, she thought to herself. She needed to land the plane right now!

She lowered the nose of the bird, aiming for the long stretch of grass. Something hard hit her in the back of the head. Pain reverberated through her skull as she blinked and struggled to keep the plane steady.

"We're going down," she cried hoarsely, as her vision blurred from the impact of being hit from behind.

"You can do it," Chris encouraged. "You've got this, Lexie!"

Lord, give me strength!

The wheels hit hard, sending more jolting pain through her head. The plane lurched to the right, the left wing rising up off the ground.

No, don't roll!

Thankfully, they weren't going fast enough to flip

the plane, but they did come to an abrupt halt, the sound of metal crunching against metal far from reassuring.

"I've got him," Chris said with satisfaction. "You did it, Lexie! We've got him."

She blew out a breath, released her death-like grip on the stick and turned in her seat. Sure enough, between Teddy and Chris, they'd overpowered Lanier enough to wrench his gun away. The man's wrists were cuffed behind him, making him no longer a threat.

To anyone, ever again.

"I'll get you for this," Lanier shouted. "You won't get away, you'll see!"

"Shut up," Chris commanded. "Frank Lanier, you're under arrest for the murder of the deputy from the transport van, the murder of Skip Taylor and kidnapping Lexie. You have the right to remain silent. Anything you say can and will be used in a court of law."

Chris went through the entire Miranda rights as she drew in several ragged breaths, while silently thanking God for keeping them all safe. She lifted a hand to her bruised head, then pushed the door open to jump down from the cockpit. Her knees almost buckled, but she managed to keep herself upright.

They'd managed to survive, but her plane hadn't fared nearly as well. Both rear tires were flatter than pancakes, and the tip of the right wing had been ripped off. She carried one spare tire, but not two.

They were stranded here outside the Lewis and Clark Caverns, without a way to get out.

At that moment a loud rumble of thunder echoed. Lexie remembered that the weather forecast had included storms in the afternoon, not now.

Looking up at the dark clouds overhead, she sighed.

The storm was moving in faster than anticipated. Her plane may function as a beacon for the lightning that often accompanied a major thunderstorm.

If that happened, they'd be forced to seek shelter in the caves.

Chris was impressed with Lexie's ingenuity and bravery. The way she'd rotated her plane wings from side to side had been just enough to throw Lanier off-balance. The moment the gun wasn't pointed at her, he'd taken the opportunity to grab Lanier's wrist, wrenching it painfully backward to disarm the convict.

Teddy's growling and nipping at Lanier hadn't hurt. Lanier had shied away from the dog, avoiding Teddy's sharp teeth as the spaniel grabbed onto his shirt and pulled.

The only problem was that during the fight for their lives, Lanier had knocked heads with Lexie, which in turn had caused her to execute an emergency landing. Yet he hadn't been all that worried. He'd trusted Lexie's amazing skills to get them safely on the ground.

And she had.

They'd survived, and finally had Lanier in custody, where he belonged. Chris hauled Lanier to the nearest tree, tying him up with a length of rope from inside the plane. Teddy stayed close to his side, as if willing to take another chunk out of Lanier as needed. Chris had kept the man's wrists cuffed, taking another moment to bind his ankles as well.

When he was finished, he looked down at the guy with satisfaction.

There was no way he'd allow this man to escape ever again.

"Good boy, Teddy." He spent a moment praising his partner for a job well done. He didn't use the bear reward, because that was only for identifying the correct scent. Still, Teddy leaned against him, as if understanding the danger they'd been in.

Chris pulled out his phone to call Ben, sighing when he realized he had no service. He put it away, noticing Lexie staring glumly at the plane.

"Is it as bad as it looks?" He came over to stand beside her.

"Yeah, I'm afraid so." She blew out a breath and turned toward him. "Unfortunately, we're not going to be able to fly out of here."

"I'd call my brother, but there's no service. Hopefully he was able to get a plane up in the air to come look for us." Chris hadn't been bluffing about that, although he had no way of knowing if Ben had managed to remain conscious long enough to request a rescue.

He silently prayed that God would watch over Ben and Shadow. Seeing them lying on the ground, drugged, had been terrifying. He was thankful the Narcan had worked to revive them. Also, his removing the darts so quickly may have helped, too.

His actions had been guided by pure instinct. And maybe by God.

For the first time since his mother's death, he realized Lexie had been right about God watching over them.

Was she also right about forgiveness? He grimaced and shied away from that thought. This wasn't the time to think about his relationship with Lexie. He needed to get Lanier back into a jail cell, and for that they'd need another plane.

"Are Ben and Shadow really okay?" Lexie asked. "I can't believe Lanier got his hands on a tranquilizer gun."

"It's probably the only weapon he could buy without getting a background check and really, it's the best weapon to use against a K-9 cop," he explained. Then he frowned. "Something I should have anticipated and been prepared for. I'm sure that tranq gun was meant for me and Teddy, only Ben and Shadow were hit, instead."

"Stop it, Chris. You can't think of every single possible scenario," she protested.

"As a cop, it's my job to do just that. To consider every and all possibilities." He appreciated Lexie's support, but if anything bad had happened to Ben or Shadow, he wouldn't have been able to forgive himself. Especially since it was his fault they'd been there in the first place. He glanced down at Teddy, who sat patiently beside him. "Drugs are one threat that can be used successfully against our dogs, and they can be difficult to avoid."

"I can understand that, but how could you know Lanier would get his hands on a dart gun?" She glanced over to where Lanier was tied to the tree. "He wouldn't have had money to buy it. I'm surprised the local cops hadn't alerted you to the theft."

"Yeah." He thought about the partial fingerprint on the scrap of paper that he now knew listed the coordinates to the caves in the mountain behind them. Lexie's plane had sustained damage landing here under extreme circumstances. But it was possible that a plane could be damaged even while executing a landing in a normal situation. "Remember that replacement tire invoice you found in Harry's files?"

"Yes." Her green gaze grew serious as she looked

once more at her lopsided plane. "You think Harry brought someone here just a few days ago?"

"If there's really money hidden inside, then yeah, someone had to have been brought here recently. Maybe a couple of trips."

"I don't want to believe Harry is involved in this," Lexie whispered.

He couldn't help himself from wrapping his arm around her shoulders. "I know it's hard, but we'll figure things out."

A roar of thunder drowned out the last part of his sentence. He looked up at the dark clouds moving in, and realized they weren't out of danger yet.

"You'll need to take Lanier into the cave," she said. "We can't leave him out here."

He hated to admit she was right. "I will, soon. I'm going to walk out from the mountain to see if I can get a phone signal."

"Hurry," she urged.

"Take cover," he advised, before jogging away from the side of the mountain.

The storm clouds swirled overhead. Instead of taking cover, Lexie pulled items from the plane, including his backpack and other tools and supplies. Then she disappeared into the cave opening.

As he ran, he stared down at his phone. Still no bars. He went as far as he dared, before realizing it was useless.

There was no way to call his brother.

He spun and turned to the cave. He pocketed his phone and pulled out his penknife. Crossing over to Lanier, he cut through the bindings that kept him up against the tree. "Get up," he said.

"You need to release my ankles, too," Lanier whined. "I can't walk."

Chris considered this dilemma for all of two seconds. "You won't have to walk, I'm going to carry you."

"What?" Lanier looked horrified, but Chris didn't care. He grabbed Lanier's bound wrists, and hefted the large, stinky man up and over his shoulders. As tempting as it was to force the man to have a rain shower to ease the smell, he carried him through the cave opening.

After dropping Lanier to the ground, he straightened. "Behave, or I'll put you outside in the storm," he threatened.

"Guess no one is coming to rescue you now, huh?" Lanier taunted.

Chris sighed. Maybe he should cut a strip off his shirt to use as a gag. "Shut up, Lanier. You have the right to remain silent, remember?"

Thankfully, Lanier clamped his lips together and looked away. Relieved, Chris took a moment to look around the interior of the cave. He noticed the supplies Lexie had neatly stacked against the wall.

He frowned. Where was Lexie, anyway? Had she gone farther into the cave?

There was a tunnel leading deeper into the mountain. He strained to listen, thinking Lexie may have gone to explore a bit, but he didn't hear anything above the thunderstorm outside.

"Lexie?"

No answer. He tightened his grip on his gun, fear returning with a vengeance.

Where was she?

Lexie hugged the cavern wall, listening intently. After seeking refuge from the storm in the cave, she thought she'd glimpsed a flash of light.

But now there was only darkness. She could hear the

dripping of water, either from deep within the cavern or from some source of rain. She wondered if the terrifying flight she'd been forced to undergo at gunpoint had caused her imagination to run wild. She didn't understand how Chris could be a cop. This constant suspecting people day in and day out was an awful way to live.

It made her understand why Chris valued honesty so much.

There!

Another flicker of light winked at her from the darkness. She wasn't losing her marbles. She edged farther along the cavern wall trying to figure out what the light was from. Lanier said something about money, and it occurred to her that he may have stashed it in the tunnel, attaching a beacon to the bag to make it easier to find.

With the thunderstorm raging outside, she thought the light might be lightning flashing from some opening in the side of the mountain. These tunnels wound around seemingly in circles and there was more than one entry and exit point.

Yes, the more she considered that option, the more convinced she was that the flash of light was from lightning. If the money was stashed in here someplace, she doubted any sort of battery-powered light would have lasted this long.

Just as she was about to turn back, she heard a noise. She froze, imagining a large animal that was using the cavern as a lair.

Moving as silently as possible, she took a step back. A flash of bright light came out of nowhere, blinding her. Lexie instinctively put a hand up to shield her eyes, when she heard a familiar voice.

"Hey, sis. About time you got here."

Jeremy? She blinked, trying to see him more clearly, but he still held the light aiming directly at her face. "Jeremy, what are you doing here?"

"Waiting for you." He reached out and roughly grabbed her arm, yanking her off-balance and forcing her deeper into the cave. She opened her mouth to scream, but he must have sensed her intent because he hissed, "Don't say a word or I'll shoot whoever comes rushing to your rescue."

Shoot? He had a gun? Why? What was going on? Was this really about money?

Then the full realization hit hard. Her brother was working with Lanier! That photograph she'd found on the internet flashed in her mind. Jeremy was probably the guy standing beside Lanier. And her brother had likely helped the convict escape from the prison van.

Lexie kept her mouth clamped shut, hoping, praying Jeremy wouldn't shoot her. At least he hadn't so far.

What had he said? Something about how he'd been waiting for her? For what? He obviously wanted something.

"Where's Frank?" he asked in a harsh whisper.

"I knocked him out." She wasn't going to let her brother know about Chris and Teddy.

"Good, saved me the trouble," Jeremy said. "Despite our little agreement, I wasn't planning on sharing any of the cash with him, anyway."

Cold. He was so cold and callous. Was her brother always like this? Or had he gotten worse in the years she'd been away?

She didn't remember Jeremy being mean to her, but as five years her senior, they hadn't spent much time together.

"How did you find me?" she finally asked.

"Did you really think you could sic the SEC on us? On me and Uncle Ron?" He laughed without humor, the sound lifting the tiny hairs on the back of her neck. "I have a contact within the SEC. He foiled your attempts to turn us over to the authorities."

She swallowed hard. Now she understood why no arrests had been made.

"I'll admit, it wasn't easy to track you down, sis," Jeremy continued. "Nice job changing your name and flying beneath the radar for so long." He laughed again. "Flying under the radar, get it?"

She didn't respond to his lame attempt at humor, her brain stuck on what he'd said. "Wait a minute, you and Uncle Ron? Not Dad? Dad told me to drop it or else."

"Oh, our father suspected something was up," Jeremy confirmed. "I think he told you that because he didn't want you in the middle of things. But he called me after you confronted him with the inconsistencies you uncovered." Jeremy's expression turned hard. "I managed to convince him you were wrong. And I'm the one who hired that guy to come after you. That idiot should have killed you, but you managed to get away."

Jeremy. All this time, she'd reported her father for being a crook, when in reality it had been her brother.

And her uncle.

Her own brother had tried to kill her.

Think, Lexie. Think! You have to figure out a way out of this mess.

She stumbled over a rock, nearly falling on her face as Jeremy took her around yet another bend in the cave tunnel. How much time had passed? Sooner or later,

Chris and Teddy would realize she was missing and come to find her.

Then again, Jeremy had a gun. If her brother had helped Lanier escape, he wouldn't hesitate to shoot another cop.

The idea of Chris or Teddy being killed made her sick to her stomach. She didn't want to be responsible for either of them getting hurt.

"So why do you need me?" Lexie forced the question past her tight throat. If Jeremy hoped she'd fly him out of there, he'd be sorely disappointed. There was no way she'd get the bird up in the air after that crash landing.

"I need you to sign over your trust fund." Jeremy's demand shouldn't have been a surprise, but it was. She'd barely thought about the trust fund she'd left behind. The fund had been started by her paternal grandfather, and she'd been concerned that her dad may have learned his criminal ways from his father, tainting that money, too.

"You have your own trust fund," she protested as he pushed her back against the wall and faced her, lowering the flashlight so that it wasn't shining directly into her eyes. "What's the problem? Don't tell me you plowed through your entire inheritance already?"

"No, I've added to my bank account over the years," Jeremy said smugly. "I have more money than our parents."

She stared at him. "Then why are you here?"

"I want more." Jeremy's eyes were bright with greed. "And you living out here in the boondocks means you won't miss your trust fund."

He was right about that. She didn't miss the money. But she was still trying to wrap her mind around what he was saying. "I'm surprised you didn't just forge my signature."

"I would have," he admitted, "if not for the fact that I'm left-handed and you're not. They have handwriting experts checking these things out now, so no. Unfortunately, forgery wasn't an option."

She hadn't paid much attention to the fact that there would have been a handwriting expert fail-safe. Still, she couldn't believe he'd done all of this just to get her here to the caves. "If you have so much money, Jeremy, why help bust Frank Lanier out of jail? Why go to the lengths of convincing him to find me? To force me to fly him here? You could have paid anyone to do that."

Jeremy stared at her with disgust. "You're not very smart, are you, sis? I've been planning my exit strategy for well over two years. I used Frank Lanier and Brett Corea to pad my bank account figuring no one would suspect me of being linked to Montana in any way, only Frank was stupid enough to get greedy, killing Brett for his portion of the money. Which he then hid here in the caves." Disgust rang in his tone.

Keep him talking. "I have to admit, I didn't realize it was your idea to have the banker embezzle money from the wealthy ranchers located along the Rocky Mountains."

"Why not?" Jeremy's eyes gleamed. "The more money, the better, right?"

Not right, she thought. Nothing about this scenario was right. It was all horribly, terribly wrong. She tried to stay on track, to get as much information from her brother as possible. "But how are you going to explain this increase in wealth once you get back to New York?"

"That's the beauty of my long-term plan." She itched to wipe the smirk from his face. "I'm not going back. With the money Frank stole from Brett and stashed here, your trust fund and mine, not to mention all the other cash I've amassed over the years, I'll have enough to live in the lap of luxury in Rio de Janeiro for the rest of my life."

A chill snaked down her spine. Rio de Janeiro? That was all the way down in South America. Didn't they have a big drug problem down there? Or was that what Jeremy was counting on? "Listen, you need to know that my plane won't carry enough fuel for us to get that far."

"Oh, you'll get me there, sis. You should be able to fly us to Canada, and from there I can easily take another plane to my ultimate destination. Your idea of changing your name helped me in that regard. I have a fake identity all set up, including a beautiful brand-new passport."

She swallowed hard, realizing her brother really had built up a substantial plan over the past two years. She resisted the urge to glance back at the tunnels they'd recently come through.

How long would it take for Chris and Teddy to notice her absence?

And even then, finding her in the maze of tunnels wouldn't be easy.

"Here's the paperwork I need you to sign." Jeremy opened a laptop case and removed several documents.

"Fine, let's get this over with." She didn't care so much about letting him have the trust fund. But the fact that he'd so callously stole from people, killing those who got into his way, was frightening.

Would Jeremy really be satisfied living the life of luxury in South America? Or would he eventually go back to his lying, scheming ways?

Their respective trust funds were each worth over

two million dollars. To her way of thinking, that wasn't nearly enough money for Jeremy to live the rest of his life in luxury, the way he claimed.

Besides, she didn't think Jeremy would stop cheating. Just watching his facial expressions as he boasted about his accomplishments made her realize just how much he thrived on all of this. He enjoyed getting his way, taking money that didn't belong to him, and ruthlessly trampling over those who stood in his path.

No, she didn't think he'd give up lying, cheating or stealing. Not now, not ever.

There had to be a way to stop him. Without anyone getting hurt. Only she couldn't report him to the authorities if she were dead.

"Take the pen."

She reached out to take the pen with trembling fingers, while she silently prayed for God to give her the strength, courage and wisdom to escape.

Something was wrong.

Chris had searched for Lexie in a few of the tunnels closest to the main area where he'd left Lanier, without finding a trace of her. He tried to tell himself that Lexie may have simply gotten lost in her quest to explore the cave but didn't really believe it.

Lexie had instantly known the latitude and longitude of the caverns, which meant she was more familiar with this landmark than he was. Besides, what could she have been searching for? Water? There was plenty of rainwater coming down. In fact, he'd left Teddy's collapsible bowl out to capture enough water to sustain them for a few hours.

No, he knew deep in his bones that something was definitely wrong.

He returned to the cave opening and stared out at the deluge falling from the sky, soaking the earth. The plane looked pathetic leaning to one side. He needed something of Lexie's to use for Teddy to track.

His gaze landed on the pack of supplies she'd brought in from the plane. Kneeling beside it, he rummaged through the contents. There was a first-aid kit full of supplies that might come in handy at some point, along with tools and random engine parts that he assumed she must know how to use. When he found a flare gun, he tucked that into his own pack to use as a backup weapon if needed, before continuing to poke through the contents. There had to be something in there that would carry Lexie's scent.

Something personal. Like clothing. Shoes were great, as people generally didn't wash them.

Dogs loved stinky feet.

When he got down to the bottom of the pack, he found a pair of worn leather gloves. He carefully pulled them out, hoping they didn't belong to Skip.

Holding one of them up to his hand, he noticed it was very small. Not large enough even for the slender mechanic, in his estimation.

The gloves had to belong to Lexie.

Not as good as shoes, but close. Drawing an evidence bag from his pack, he carefully dropped both gloves inside. He was glad to have a way to find Lexie but continued pulling items from the bag.

He'd need to mark the cave as he and Teddy went through the tunnels, or they'd all end up lost in there. He found a fat stick of white chalk and tucked that into his pocket. Between the chalk and his penknife, he'd be able to mark his route as he searched for Lexie.

There was a half-empty water bottle in the bag, too, so he took that for Teddy. Then he brought in the collapsible water bowl, encouraging his partner to drink before they headed out.

When he was finally ready, Chris led Teddy deep into the cave, away from Lanier's prying eyes.

He'd ended up using a strip of fabric to tie around his mouth, to shut the guy up. He kept talking about money, and how Chris didn't understand what he was up against.

The cop in him wanted nothing more than for the idiot to keep talking, but listening to his rambling got old real fast. Now he was glad the guy couldn't talk about what he and Teddy were about to do.

"This is Lexie," he said, offering Teddy the scent bag. "Lexie. Seek Lexie!"

Teddy's big brown eyes peered up at him, seeming to understand the gravity of the situation. His partner stuck his nose into the bag for long minutes, then turned and went to work.

Chris decided to keep him on leash. For one thing, he'd need to stop to mark their route, and for another, he just had a bad feeling about this.

Chris had assumed that Harry was Lanier's accomplice. But what if he was wrong? The convict had basically announced he was holding Lexie at gunpoint to fly here to the caves for the money. But what if there was more to it?

What if there wasn't just money here, but someone else who also wanted the money?

Harry? The guy hadn't flown here, when he so easily could have. Which made him think there may be someone else.

Another accomplice. One who didn't have a criminal record but had left a partial print on the slip of paper he'd found under Skip's workbench. Coordinates for the caverns. Lexie's father?

Teddy lifted his nose to the air and trotted down a tunnel. When the dog made a turn, Chris held him back until he could make a small white arrow with the chalk, indicating the direction they'd gone.

"Seek Lexie," he commanded in a whisper.

Teddy continued following a path only he could smell. When they came to yet another Y in the tunnel, he told Teddy to heel, as he once again used the chalk to mark the wall.

Teddy tugged on the leash impatiently. Chris took that as a good sign that he was following Lexie's scent.

They made it halfway down the next tunnel when the low murmur of voices reached his ears. He pulled Teddy to a stop, bent down and gently clasped his hand over the dog's snout to prevent him from making any noise.

"Here, are you happy now? You have full control over my trust fund." Lexie's voice was so quiet he could barely hear her. He frowned as he tried to make sense of what she was saying.

What trust fund?

"It's a start," a male voice responded. "Now you're going to fly me out of here."

"I might not have enough fuel to get you all the way to Canada," Lexie said. "I mean, I only had enough fuel for a tour. I didn't fill the fuel tank for a trip over the border."

Canada? Chris didn't like where this conversation

was going. And who was Lanier's accomplice? Gerald Hall? He wished he'd taken the time to interrogate Frank, but finding Lexie had been a higher priority.

"You better get me there, sis. Failure is not an option."

Sis? The photograph that Russ sent him featuring Gerald, Abigail, Savannah and Jeremy flashed in his mind.

Lexie had been betrayed by her own brother.

Chris gently pushed Teddy behind him, giving the hand signal for quiet, as he considered his options. He had his service weapon, and the flare gun. They might need the flare gun to get a search plane in the area, so he'd use that only as a last resort.

He heard movement and quickly rose to his feet. Remembering the last Y in the tunnel, he quickly led Teddy back to that spot, going partway down the path he hadn't marked. He kept the dog positioned behind him. Teddy wasn't a protector like Ben's Doberman, Shadow, but he would still lunge at anyone who tried to harm him.

He didn't want anything to happen to Teddy or to Lexie.

Hopefully, using the element of surprise, he'd be able to get Lexie away from her brother. Chris drew in a deep breath, trying to calm his racing heart. He had to assume Jeremy was armed, the way Lanier had been.

A gun Jeremy wouldn't hesitate to use against his own flesh and blood.

Chris's chest hurt, it was difficult to breathe. He cared about Lexie. Savannah. Whatever she chose to call herself.

He lifted his heart in prayer. *Lord, give me the strength I need to save Lexie!*

And waited.

FIFTEEN

Lexie didn't know where Chris and Teddy were, or if they even realized she was being held hostage by her brother. She'd thought she'd heard something moving in the tunnel and had tried to distract Jeremy.

But she hadn't heard anything more. Nor had she seen any sign of Chris or his K-9 partner.

Now Jeremy was pushing her ahead of him, holding the gun on her back as he lugged the large duffel bag full of money. She wasn't sure how much cash would fit in a duffel bag that size, but she sensed that Jeremy didn't care about the exact amount. He simply wanted everything he could get his greedy hands on.

And once she'd taken him to Canada, he'd have no use for her.

She moved slowly and carefully through the cave, the light bouncing around as Jeremy held the flashlight behind her. Several times she tripped over stalagmites and other rocks scattered along the floor of the cave but managed to stay upright.

What would Jeremy do when he saw her damaged plane? She had no doubt he'd take his anger out on her, even though this entire money-grabbing scheme was his idea in the first place.

She was glad her father hadn't tried to kill her. Not that learning Jeremy had been responsible for sending that man to her apartment made her feel much better. Yet, somehow, it was easier to accept Jeremy's duplicity more so than her own father's.

And her uncle Ron? Did Jeremy plan to leave him behind to take the fall for the embezzling?

"Hurry up," Jeremy said harshly. "I want to get out of this place."

"Strange place to hide cash, don't you think?" Lexie kept talking, hoping that Chris and Teddy would hear them coming. "How did you get here, anyway?"

"I got a ride. You're not the only pilot in the area," Jeremy said. "If not for needing your signature on your trust fund, I would have used the old guy to get out of here."

Harry, she thought. He must be referring to Harry. His bringing Jeremy here must be when his wheel had gone flat. "But that means you've been here for several days," she said, thinking out loud.

"Yeah, way longer than planned," Jeremy said flatly. "Lanier was supposed to have brought you here two days ago."

"That's what happens when you put your trust in a convict," she shot back.

The muzzle of his gun poked her hard, causing her to stumble. This time, the tip of her shoe hit a large rock. She couldn't catch herself, hitting the ground, hard.

A rush of movement had her instinctively rolling away as Chris lunged at Jeremy from the shadows.

"He's got a gun," she shouted to Chris in warning.

The two men tumbled to the earth. The flashlight Jeremy had been carrying fell to the ground. She scrambled on her hands and knees to pick it up, playing the light on the two men.

Their hands were locked on the gun, the barrel pointing at the cave ceiling. Feeling panicked, she cast her gaze around. She found the rock she'd stumbled over and set the flashlight on the ground, with the beam of light pointing upward, so that she could edge closer to hit Jeremy on the back of his head.

The gun barrel swung toward her. Undeterred, she sidestepped, positioning herself so she was behind her brother. In the beam of the flashlight, she could see Chris fighting Jeremy for the gun.

The muzzle of the weapon wavered, then pointed upward again. There was a millisecond when she saw the back of Jeremy's head. Moving quickly, she brought the rock down hard against his skull.

Her brother howled and let go of the gun. Chris yanked it away and then roughly pushed him over. Her brother slumped face-first on the ground.

Something soft brushed her leg as Teddy darted past, latching on to Jeremy's ankle. The dog growled low in his throat, but Jeremy didn't move.

"Lexie? Are you okay?" Chris's voice sounded as if it were at the end of a long tunnel. At some point she was aware that Chris had bound Jeremy's wrists behind his back, the same way he'd tied up Lanier.

She looked down at the bloodstained rock she still held in her hand and instantly dropped it, wiping her palm against her dusty jeans.

She'd struck her own brother. Knocked him unconscious.

What if she'd killed him?

"Lexie?" Chris stepped over the duffel bag and gently cupped her shoulders. "You're okay. Take a deep breath. We're okay."

"I-is he dead?" Her voice was a hoarse whisper.

"No, he's alive. That's why I bound his wrists." Chris pulled her into his arms. "I'm sorry you had to do that, but I'm glad you're not hurt."

It seemed like eons since Chris had cradled her in his arms. She gratefully clung to him, burying her face in the hollow of his shoulder. "All Jeremy wanted was money. He didn't care about anything else. Especially me. Thank you for saving my life."

"Oh, Lexie. I think you saved mine," he murmured, his mouth near her ear. "God was watching over both of us today."

"Yes, He was." Ridiculous tears pricked her eyelids. She was glad she hadn't killed Jeremy, even though she knew that he would have ended her life without hesitating one second.

"We should get out of here," Chris finally said. "I don't know about you, but braving a thunderstorm is better than being stuck in the depths of this cave."

"Okay." She forced herself to loosen her grip. The flashlight she'd set on the ground offered enough illumination to see the concern etched in Chris's features. "Let's go."

"Lexie." Chris said her name on a sigh. Then he pulled her close again and kissed her.

The embrace was all too brief. Jeremy let out a low groan, interrupting them.

"Good, you're waking up," Chris said. He squeezed

her hand, then moved over to her brother. "Now I don't have to carry you out. You can walk."

Jeremy moaned again, rolling onto his back. He blinked as he stared up at her. "You hit me!"

"At least I didn't kill you." The words came out of her mouth before she could stop them. "Which is more than I can say about what your plans were for me."

A feral expression creased his face, before he began to whine. "You know I was only bluffing, Savannah. I only wanted you to cooperate with me. You're family. I could never kill you."

"Yeah, sing another tune," she advised. The flash of anger was Jeremy's true nature, not this *woe is me* routine he was playing up.

"On your feet," Chris said, yanking Jeremy upright. "Jeremy Hall, you're under arrest for assault with a deadly weapon, embezzlement, attempted murder of a police officer and whatever other charges I can come up with once I understand the full extent of your crimes."

Lexie went over to pick up the duffel. It was heavier than she anticipated. Following Chris and Jeremy, she took some solace in the fact that they could return this money to the bank and to the ranchers who'd been swindled by Corea, Jeremy and Lanier.

The danger was finally over.

Now all they had to do was wait for the storm to pass, so the rescue plane could pick them up.

When they reached the cave entrance, she glanced at Chris, wondering if this was the last time she'd ever see him.

His case was over. He'd successfully arrested Lanier, and her brother, too.

She couldn't imagine her life without him, even

though she knew Chris would be relieved to leave her and Great Falls, Montana, behind.

Forever.

"Stay there," Chris said as he pushed Jeremy over to the wall of the cave opening. Outside, he noticed the clouds had moved past, taking the rain with them. As suddenly as the storm had come upon them, it had swept away.

It was good to know the rescue plane could head in now, that the storm had dissipated. If Ben had been able to arrange for one.

Teddy began to growl, low in his throat. Chris straightened, trying to understand what was bothering his partner.

One glance at Lanier made him frown. He'd left the escaped convict sitting just inside the cave opening, but now he was lying awkwardly on his side in the dirt, his hands still bound behind his back. Lanier didn't move, and from this angle, Chris couldn't even tell if the guy was breathing. He hadn't tied the gag that tightly. He should have been able to breathe.

A trap? Maybe. He wouldn't put anything past Lanier, or Lexie's brother, for that matter. Chris pulled his weapon and gave Teddy the hand signal to sit and stay. "Lanier? Sit up and face me."

Nothing.

He took several steps forward, then froze. The convict's throat was gaping open from a jagged wound, a pool of blood soaking the earth beneath him.

There was no doubt in his mind, the guy was dead.

No! Chris spun around, a second too late. A middle-aged man emerged from the brush outside the cave opening, holding a shotgun. "Throw down your weapon," the stranger said. "Or I'll start shooting. From this distance I can hit Savannah and the dog without even trying."

Savannah?

"Uncle Ron?" Lexie's voice came out as a high squeak. "What are you doing here?"

Uncle Ron? Chris considered the photo he'd seen of Lexie's family, and remembered the computer screen image of Gerald and Ron Hall supporting the New York City mayoral candidate.

First her brother, now her uncle. Her father, too? Hard to believe how messed up Lexie's family was. This made his mother's lie seem like nothing.

No wonder Lexie had changed her name and moved to Great Falls, Montana. He'd treated her unfairly, comparing her to Debra and his mother in his mind.

"Your stupid brother thought he could steal from me and get away with it." Ron laughed harshly.

"You followed me, old man?" Jeremy asked from his perch against the wall.

"I knew you'd go after Savannah to get your hands on her trust fund. So yeah, I followed you."

Jeremy muttered a curse. "You should have told me your plan, Unc. We could have escaped together."

"Yeah right." Ron snorted. "You're not as smart as you think you are, Jeremy." The older man's gaze sharpened on Chris. "Drop your weapon. Now!"

Chris slowly complied with the request. He was tempted to rush the guy. After all, how much did a stockbroker know about firing a shotgun? Then again, the guy looked mighty comfortable standing there with the weapon. No, Chris didn't dare risk Lexie or Teddy getting hurt.

"How did you get here?" Chris asked. From where he stood, he couldn't see anything other than the lop-sided wings of Lexie's damaged bird. Being deep in the cavern for so long, there had been no way to hear a plane approaching. Whoever had flown Ron Hall here must have left the hangar the moment the storm moved out of the area.

Did that mean the rescue plane was on its way, too? Maybe.

Please, Lord, please keep us all safe in Your care!

"Oh, I have a pilot and a plane." A poor facsimile of a smile creased the older man's features. "He wasn't exactly happy to oblige, but I convinced him he didn't have a choice. And his plane is in much better condition than Savannah's."

"I'm sorry, Lexie. So sorry," a male voice said.

Chris noticed a man had come out from behind Ron Hall. Judging by his white hair, Chris figured he was Harry Olson, the owner of Blue Skye Aviation. He was a little older than Skip, at least by appearance. And Chris couldn't help but wonder if Harry had been in this whole thing from the very beginning.

"Toss the duffel over here, Savannah," Ron said. When she hesitated, he scowled and barked, "Now!"

"Fine. You can have it," Lexie said with disgust. She picked up the duffel and chucked it toward him. It had been too heavy for her and landed several feet short of where the man stood. "I'm glad my father isn't involved in this. Your greed will be your downfall, Uncle Ron."

"What do you care?" Ron took two steps forward

until the duffel was beside him. "You're living off the grid in the middle of nowhere, Montana."

"Yet here you are," Lexie countered. "Right in the middle of nowhere, Montana, with me. Do you honestly think you'll get away with this?"

"Yes, I do." Ron smirked, seeming to have no shortage of confidence. "And you helped tremendously by taking care of Jeremy for me."

"Wait, you can't leave me here," Jeremy protested. "Come on, take me with you." He pushed away from the wall and took a few staggering steps forward. "Please, Uncle Ron. I helped you fool my father. You owe me this much."

"I owe you nothing!" Ron's shout startled Teddy. The dog jumped and began to growl again. "You stole from me, Jeremy. Did you honestly think I didn't pick up on the wire transfers you made from my account?"

"I'm sorry, but hey, that's water under the bridge. We can start over someplace new," Jeremy whined. "We made a great team, didn't we?"

"You don't know the meaning of the word *team*," Ron spat.

While uncle and nephew argued, Chris carefully slid forward a couple of inches. He didn't have a solid plan, other than to disarm Ron Hall.

Harry must have noticed his movement, because the owner of Blue Skye Aviation crept closer to Ron as well. Maybe the old pilot wasn't part of this. Chris gave the guy an almost imperceptible nod, encouraging him to continue. Between the two of them, they might be able to catch Ron off guard long enough to make a play for the gun.

Chris still had the flare gun in his pack. He also had

a gun in his ankle holster. Ron must not have known that most cops carry a second clutch piece, exactly for this type of situation.

But he couldn't grab either weapon without drawing Ron's attention.

"I'll sign over Savannah's trust fund to you," Jeremy went on. "That's another two million."

Two million? Chris tried not to react at that amount of money. Instead, he kept his gaze focused on Ron, judging the distance between them. Not close enough to avoid getting shot if he couldn't disarm the guy. He and Teddy were wearing bullet-resistant vests, but Lexie wasn't.

And at this close range, he wasn't convinced the vest would protect him, anyway.

Still, it was a risk he'd have to take. The longer this went on, the more likely someone was going to get hurt. Chris edged forward another couple of inches. He quickly glanced at Lexie, trying to urge her to back up away from her uncle.

She didn't seem to understand.

The two men were still bickering; mostly Jeremy was pleading for his uncle to take him along. The distraction worked to Chris's advantage.

"Shut up!" Ron abruptly shouted. At that moment, Harry leaped forward, pushing the guy hard in the center of the back. The moment Harry moved to shove Ron, Chris leaped forward. He closed the gap between them, using all his strength to knock the shotgun up and out of the man's hands.

The gun belched loudly as Ron reflexively pulled the trigger. Chris didn't dare check on Lexie, hoping and praying she hadn't been hit.

"Nooo," Ron shouted as Chris roughly yanked the gun from his grip. He slammed the butt of the shotgun against Ron's shoulder, forcing him to the ground.

Harry wasn't finished. He jumped on Ron's back, holding him down. "He made me fly him here at gunpoint," Harry said between huffing breaths.

"I know." Chris turned and stared at Lexie. "Are you okay?"

Her face pale, she nodded.

"Here." He handed the shotgun to Lexie. "Don't hesitate to fire if one of them tries to escape."

She nodded jerkily, but he suspected she'd never fired a gun in her life, and likely wasn't going to start now. But these guys didn't need to know that. He hurried over to Lanier's dead body, pulling the ropes from his wrists to use on Ron Hall.

"You can move off him now, Harry," Chris said. "I'm a police officer. I can take it from here."

Harry shifted off Ron just enough for Chris to tie the older man's wrists together.

"A cop?" Ron sputtered, his face red. "You idiot," he screamed at Jeremy. "You let yourself get caught by a cop?"

"You did, too," Jeremy shot back. "And you're the idiot. You were outnumbered from the beginning. If you'd have cut me loose, we would have been able to team up, even things out. We could have gotten away. This is all your fault!"

"Be quiet, Jeremy," Lexie said. "You, too, Uncle Ron."

"I can gag them if necessary," Chris offered. "I'm tired of listening to Jeremy whine, anyway."

Lexie let out a choked laugh. "Yeah, me, too." She pointed the gun at her brother. "How does it feel to know you're heading to jail? Maybe you and our dear uncle Ron will get to share a jail cell. Wouldn't that be fun?"

Jeremy opened his mouth to respond, then likely thought better of it. Especially when Chris pulled out a roll of gauze. "This should work well as a gag, don't you think?" he asked Lexie.

"Perfect."

The rumble of a plane engine reached their ears. Chris looked up at the sky. The plane wasn't close, so he reached for the flare gun.

"Hold on, Chris, no need to use the flare. We have Harry's plane."

"Uh, not exactly." Harry grimaced. "I landed the plane hard. To be honest, it doesn't look much better than yours, Lexie."

"Oh no," Lexie moaned. "That's not good."

Chris quickly lifted the flare gun and fired. The flare shot into the sky in a blaze of orange.

But the rescue plane kept going in the opposite direction. Leaving them behind.

SIXTEEN

Lexie's shoulders slumped as the rescue plane veered off course, disappearing from view.

"They'll be back," Chris said encouragingly. He pulled out his phone. "This wouldn't work earlier, and it looks like I have one bar. What about you, Lexie?"

She looked down at her phone. "I've got nothing." Then an idea occurred to her. "But the radio on the plane should work."

"Smart," Chris said with a grin. "See if you can get a hold of someone who can request the rescue plane to turn around and come back."

"I'll do my best." She turned and quickly strode toward the planes. Harry's plane was only about fifty yards from hers. Despite what he'd said, his didn't look nearly as badly damaged as hers.

She tried her radio first. The connection was crackly, making it difficult to hear. She glanced through the windshield, noting the stretch of grass they'd been forced to use as a runway was between two mountains.

Was it possible the mountains were interfering with the radio frequency?

Frustrated, she jumped out of her plane and went

over to Harry's. Her stomach knotted when she experienced the same result.

Sliding out and onto the ground, she peered beneath Harry's plane. His was a newer-model Cessna, but maybe, just maybe, they could use parts from her plane to fix his.

"Harry!" She ran back to the cave entrance. "The radio isn't going through, but I think we can still fly out of here."

"How?" Harry demanded.

"We need to fix your plane with stuff from mine." She glanced at Chris. "Unless you've gotten through to Ben?"

"I tried, but the connection wasn't good. I can't be sure he heard me." Chris frowned as she gathered things together. "Are you really going to try to repair the plane?"

"Yeah, I am." She glanced at him. "Harry's plane isn't nearly as beat up as mine."

Chris nodded. "I believe you can do anything you set your mind to, Lexie."

"Thanks for the vote of confidence." She glanced over to where Jeremy and Ron were listening sullenly. "If nothing else, we can fly out ourselves, and leave them here."

"What? You can't do that," Jeremy sputtered. "Tied up like this, we're not able to defend ourselves."

"Then be nice," she shot back. She didn't really intend to leave them behind, even though they'd planned far worse for her. Jesus taught His followers to forgive those who trespassed against you. Looking at her uncle and brother, she better understood how difficult that was when faced with being betrayed by your own family.

She hesitated, looking down at the tools. What if this didn't work?

"Hey, give it your best shot, Lexie," Chris said, reading her mind. "We can always wait for the rescue plane to return."

"We can, but what happens if another storm pops up? Or if we're still stuck here when it gets dark?" She couldn't explain the desperate need to get out of this place. Bending down, she continued gathering the tools and other supplies together into the pack she'd originally taken from her plane. "It's going to take us time to get Harry's bird ready to fly, anyway. Keep trying your phone. Maybe you'll get through."

"Okay." Chris's smile was crooked. "I'd offer to help, but I'm pretty sure I'd be more of a hindrance."

She laughed, the sound rusty. It felt strange to feel happy after everything they'd been through. "You're needed here, anyway. I don't trust either of them." She jerked her thumb toward Ron and Jeremy.

"I don't, either." Chris looked as if he wanted to say something more, but then he turned away. "Guard, Teddy. Guard."

On cue, Teddy growled low in his throat. She remembered the first time she'd met the pair, after Chris had fought with Frank Lanier, suffering a minor head injury in the process.

That seemed like months ago, rather than a handful of days.

"Come on, Harry." She slung the pack of supplies over her shoulder. "Better to get this done before the weather changes."

"For sure." Harry glanced at her as they walked back to the planes. "I'm sorry about this, Lexie. I had no idea that guy was your uncle."

"It's not your fault. How could you know something like that?" She hadn't let herself fixate on the fact that her own brother and uncle had turned into such greedy jerks. "At least my dad isn't involved, the way I thought he was over these past five years."

"Your father?" Harry blanched, but then didn't say anything more as they reached her plane.

"They both have flat tires and one broken tire rod," she said with a sigh. "But we may be able to stabilize your broken rod with a replacement from my bird."

"Yeah, I can see that," Harry agreed. He rubbed his hands together. "Let's get to work."

"I found two roles of duct tape." She pulled various items from the pack.

"Wish we had a soldering iron," he grumbled as he used a hammer to knock a pole loose. "Not sure duct tape is going to do the trick."

She shared his concern. "All we can do is try."

"Hrmph." Harry grunted as he hauled the rod over to his plane. "It's not the taking-off part I'm worried about. It's landing at the hangar."

"I know." She didn't relish that aspect of the plan, either. "But if the rescue plane doesn't swing back, soon, we'll have to give it a try. And I'll land at the main terminal rather than the hangar, so there will be help nearby in case we crash." She didn't want to be stuck in the caverns at night, with two criminals and no food. Not to mention, Lanier's dead body would attract carnivores.

She shivered. She was used to living in the wilds, but

not when there was a dead body close by to lure wild animals. The sooner they got out of here, the better.

"Help me with this," Harry instructed.

She helped hold the rod in place as he replaced the damaged one. Then she used duct tape to assist in stabilizing the repair. Stepping back, she eyed their handiwork, wondering if the rod would hold.

The good news was that Harry's Cessna now stood level. One wheel was damaged, so they exchanged that with the good wheel from her plane. Thankfully, being Cessnas, the swap went well.

Finally, Harry tinkered with the engine. When he finished, he turned to face her. "We've done what we can. She'll get us up in the air."

"We'll fly at the lowest altitude possible considering the terrain," she said, injecting confidence in her tone. "We'll make it work."

"I'd like you to be the pilot," Harry said.

"Me?" She gaped at him in surprise. She had only been flying for just under five years, compared with his thirty years of experience. "Why?"

Harry reluctantly lifted his arms. Both his hands shook in a way that made her gasp. "I didn't exactly try to land the plane rough. My shaking contributed to that. I've been diagnosed with Parkinson's disease." He lowered his hands. "You're a really good pilot, Lexie. If anyone can land this bird with the repairs we made, it's you."

Parkinson's disease? She drew in a deep breath and slowly nodded. After all, what could she say? "Okay, let's get everyone on board."

Harry gently patted her on the back. "It's going to be fine, you'll see."

Lexie took a moment to glance up at the cloudy sky. The rain had stopped, but the wind hadn't diminished as much as she'd have liked. If her landing gear was solid, yeah, she'd land the bird no problem. But with the one wheel rod replaced and basically duct-taped together? The risk of crash-landing in a way that caused the plane to roll was much higher.

She felt certain the radio would work once they were away from the mountains, but the best she could do would be to make sure an ambulance and fire truck were waiting at the hangar for them.

Just in case the landing didn't go as planned.

The responsibility for five people's lives weighed on her shoulders. There was no margin for error.

If she messed up, they could all die.

Dear Lord, please provide me the skill and strength I need to do this!

Chris held his weapon on Jeremy and Ron as the five of them walked toward the plane. He tried not to look horrified by the fact that Lexie and Harry had done some of the repair with duct tape.

Yet the rescue plane hadn't returned, and with the clouds overhead, the area outside the caves was already getting dark. The air was heavy with moisture, indicating another storm might be rolling in, too.

The howls from a pack of coyotes were too close for comfort. Coyotes were scavengers, but he knew other wildlife would soon follow. He'd dragged Lanier's body into the cave, and covered him the best he could until they could send someone to retrieve him.

In the end, Chris had agreed with Lexie's plan to fly

them out of there, rather than waiting any longer for the rescue plane to return.

Still, the duct-tape reinforcement of the wheel pole wasn't entirely reassuring. Lexie and Harry had dragged the plane over to a spot where they could make the most of the grassy runway.

Jeremy balked when it came his turn to get into the plane. "This thing is unsafe!"

"You want to stay here?" Chris shrugged. He'd shouldered the duffel bag of cash Jeremy had risked his life for, as proof of what had transpired in the caves. "Fine with me. I'm not going to force you to come along."

Jeremy looked back toward the caverns, likely remembered Lanier's dead body was there, then reluctantly sighed. "Fine. I'll go with you."

Chris had refused to untie their hands, which meant Harry had to pull Ron and Jeremy up from inside the plane, while Chris gave them a leg up. He tossed the duffel in the back, and then lifted Teddy into the plane, keeping the dog close to his side.

Finally they were settled inside the plane. Lexie was in the pilot's seat, while Harry sat beside her. The two of them looked at each other as she started the engine.

"Let's do this," she said. Chris found himself holding his breath as she increased their speed, rolling over the grassy runway.

At the last possible second, she lifted them airborne, the wheels seemingly a hair's width from the treetops. He let out his breath, secretly amazed that they'd made it this far without the wheel of the plane falling off. As they rose in elevation, he thanked God for providing Lexie the skill to keep them safe.

"Mayday, mayday, this is Lexie McDaniels of Blue Skye Aviation. Can anyone read me? Over."

Loud crackling noises filled his headset. She tried again, repeating her call for help, and finally he heard a voice respond beyond the crackling noises.

"This is the tower at Great Falls. I read you, Lexie. We're glad to hear from you, over."

"I need an ambulance on scene, along with the local police and a fire truck," Lexie said calmly. "ETA roughly fifteen minutes. I'm coming in with broken landing gear, over."

More crackling noises. "Ten-four, rescue teams will be on-site, over."

Rescue teams. Chris had prayed often since he'd jumped on board Lexie's plane earlier that morning. Now he realized the danger wasn't over. Getting up into the air was only half the battle. They still needed to land.

Hopefully without crashing.

Ironically, Chris didn't feel the same level of fear he had when Lexie had been forced to land while he and Lanier had struggled for the gun. He understood now that turning away from the church after his mother's passing had been the wrong thing to do.

God had always been there for him, especially while he was growing up. His mother worked hard, but they'd also been blessed with many wonderful people who'd helped them out.

Thinking back, he realized that those kind of people didn't have a lot of money, either, but that didn't matter. Happiness was being with others, not dollars and cents. Something Lexie's family had failed to understand.

And he wanted to be just like those people who cared and helped others when they needed it the most.

God's presence seemed to fill the interior of the plane as Lexie headed toward the Great Falls airport. The Blue Skye hangar was way off to the side of the airport, but from listening to Lexie's conversation through the headset, he understood they were landing in a different location, closer to the main part of the airport.

Through the window, he could see the red and white lights of the ambulances and fire trucks at the side of the runway down below. Lexie dropped the plane's altitude, bringing the plane closer to the unforgivable and hard surface of the landing strip.

"You're doing great, Lexie," Harry said.

"Yes, you've got this," Chris added.

Lexie didn't answer, her attention seemingly riveted on the task before her. She slowed the plane and dropped lower still.

Despite his confidence in her ability, he found himself holding his breath as the front wheel touched down first, followed by the two rear wheels. They traveled several yards before the tire rod they'd repaired collapsed. The belly of the plane hit the concrete and made a loud scraping sound as the plane's momentum carried them forward.

Finally, they came to a stop.

Thank You, Lord! Thank You!

"You did it, Lexie!" Harry shouted with glee. "I knew you would."

"Thanks, but we need to get out of the plane." Lexie ripped her headphones off and jumped out. Chris pushed his door open and slid out, while she helped Harry. Teddy followed, landing nimbly beside him.

"What about us!" Jeremy screamed. "Don't leave us here!"

Tempting, he thought. But, of course, that wasn't an option. Chris reached up and guided both bound men from the plane. Ron Hall had maintained his cool demeanor throughout the short flight, a welcome relief next to Jeremy's nonstop whining.

Dozens of firefighters came rushing forward along with a couple of ambulance crews. Lexie glanced at Chris, and he understood they needed to move away from the plane just in case the fuel tank had been damaged during the landing.

"No one is hurt," Lexie quickly informed the EMTs. "We just need to get away from the plane."

They all hurried away from the bird, while the firefighters ran toward it.

"No one is hurt, so we can leave?" one of the EMTs asked.

"No, my head hurts," Jeremy whined.

"And my chest hurts," Ron added. "I might be having a heart attack."

Chris narrowed his gaze, firmly believing this was a last-ditch effort to find an opportunity to escape. "You're not going anywhere until I have two police officers watching over you as you receive medical care," he ordered.

"Fine with me. Hey, we need cops over here," one of the EMTs shouted.

Several Great Falls police officers hurried over. "You're Chris Fuller, right?" the taller cop asked. He recognized him as Louis Howard, the cop who'd come to back him up at the abandoned house.

"Yes. Thanks for being here."

"We're glad you're safe," Howard said. He glanced at the two bound suspects. "We can take over with these guys."

"Okay, but keep in mind, they are to remain in custody at all times. They're wanted for murder, embezzlement and attempted murder of Lexie and me. Do not give them a chance to escape, understand?"

Howard exchanged a glance with his partner, before nodding grimly. "We hear you, loud and clear."

"Good." He watched as they hauled Jeremy and Ron Hall away with the EMTs in tow. Then he turned and swept Lexie into his arms. "I'm so proud of you," he whispered.

She gripped him tightly. "I was so afraid of crashing."

"You didn't show it, and God was watching over us the entire time," he murmured. "We're alive, thanks to you."

Teddy nudged his leg, but Chris couldn't take his gaze from Lexie. Beautiful, kind, brave, talented Lexie.

Not Savannah, It was obvious she'd left that woman behind when she'd relocated to Montana.

"We did it," Lexie said. "The nightmare is finally over."

"I'm glad we're safe," he whispered huskily. He wanted to kiss her again, but before he could lower his lips to hers, he heard his name.

"Chris! Chris, are you okay?" Ben rushed forward with Shadow at his side. "I'm so sorry! I hate knowing I let you down."

"We're fine," he assured his brother. "And you didn't let me down. We had no way of anticipating Lanier would use a tranq gun." He reluctantly turned from

Lexie to greet Ben. His brother gave him a one-armed hug, slapping his back. Chris returned the embrace, his throat tight with emotion. What if he had died before making amends with Ben? And what about their father? What if he also died before he could make amends with his dad?

He needed to meet with his father, very soon. But not now. There would be time for that later. At the moment, there was still plenty of work to do.

Including sending someone to pick up Lanier's body from the Lewis and Clark Caverns.

Teddy and Shadow sniffed each other, but since they were wearing their work vests, they didn't try to fight or play.

"I was so worried about you," Ben said. "I couldn't believe it when you ran after the plane and jumped inside, taking Teddy with you."

"Yeah, well, it's a good thing I did, or Lexie would be dead." He turned to find Lexie, but she was quickly walking away.

"Did you do something to make her mad?" Ben asked with a frown.

"I don't think so." He stared after her for a moment, then glanced at Ben. "I have to go. I'll catch up with you later."

A smile tugged at the corner of Ben's mouth. "You do that, bro. And thanks for not blaming me as much as I'm blaming myself."

Chris broke into a run, Teddy keeping pace beside him. "Lexie? Lexie, wait up!"

He saw her pause, then slowly turn to face him. Her smile didn't quite reach her eyes. "One of the officers informed me that I'm needed inside to provide a statement," she said.

"I know. I have to, too." He searched her gaze, trying to figure out what he'd done to make her mad. "I'd like to talk to you later."

She glanced past him to where Ben and Shadow were waiting. "I think you have other priorities, don't you? Or haven't you decided to follow God's path to forgiveness?"

"I forgive you, Lexie." He took a step closer. "I understand now why you were desperate to escape your family."

Her expression softened. "I'm glad to hear you forgive me, but what about your mother? And your father?"

He hesitated. "I don't know," he answered honestly.

She nodded. "That's what I thought. Call me when you do, and we'll talk then."

"Lexie, wait…" But it was too late.

She kept walking, without looking back.

SEVENTEEN

Leaving Chris and Teddy was the hardest thing she'd ever done. Yet Lexie knew he needed time to reconcile with his past.

Without doing that, he'd never be able to fully embrace a future.

A future that likely wouldn't include her. Her chest hurt so badly, she put a hand over her sternum, wondering if this was what a broken heart felt like.

"Lexie!" She paused when she heard Harry's voice. "Wait up."

She turned to face Harry. "I owe you my life," he said.

"That's not true. You did your part in getting us out of there." She hoped she'd never have to return to the Lewis and Clark Caverns ever again. The memories of everything that had transpired tumbled over her.

Jeremy forcing her to sign over her trust at gunpoint. Her uncle Ron threatening to kill them all. The two men arguing over the money.

It always came down to money. Frankly, she'd rather her trust fund be used to help reimburse everyone Jeremy stole from.

Darting a glance over her shoulder, she watched Chris pull the duffel bag of money from the plane and hand it over to the authorities. It was a start, and she was glad to know the money would be reimbursed to the rightful owners.

But what about what Jeremy and Ron had done? She felt certain her measly two million in her trust fund wouldn't go very far.

It was better than nothing. And maybe, once Jeremy and Ron had been convicted of their crimes, their funds, and hers, would provide some measure of compensation.

"Ms. Hall? We'd like a word with you."

She tried not to grimace when she saw two men dressed in the typical navy blue suits of the FBI. Was it possible they'd finally figured out what Jeremy and Uncle Ron had done? "Of course." She turned toward Harry. "I'll catch up with you later."

"I want to sell the hangar to you," Harry blurted. "I can't fly anymore, and I'd like you to have my planes and my hangar. If you're interested."

Her jaw went slack, but she managed to recover quickly enough. "I doubt I can afford it, but thanks for the thought, Harry."

"I'll make sure the price is right. Think about it, Lexie," Harry called out after her.

Lexie had a feeling she'd do nothing but think about his offer. It was a sweet gesture on his part. However, she really couldn't afford to buy Harry out, and her annual income wasn't enough to pay off a large loan, either. Especially since she'd need money to repair her plane. Which was still sitting in front of the stupid caverns. She grimaced as she realized she'd have to go back there with a mechanic, after all.

"Ms. Hall?" the FBI agent closest to her prompted.

"My legal name is Lexie McDaniels." She followed

the two FBI agents into the closest building, another hangar much nicer than the one she rented from Harry.

The FBI agents were from the New York office, and she thought they must have been alerted by Ben and Chris's boss. Still, they kept her there for two solid hours, questioning her about what had happened five years ago in New York along with the most recent events.

When she sensed they'd keep going, she lifted her hand. "Enough. I've been cooperative and will continue to assist in any way I can. But I'm exhausted and haven't eaten all day."

"Just one more question," Special Agent Vance said. "Do you have any record of all those calls you made to the SEC over the years?"

She nodded. "I used a disposable phone that I have hidden at home. I'm happy to turn it over to you."

"Excellent, thank you. We can drive you home to get it."

Since she needed a ride anyway, she agreed. There was no reason to continue staying in the motel. Lanier was dead, and her brother and uncle had been arrested.

The danger was over.

After a quick stop to pick up her things from the motel, the FBI dropped her off at her cabin. The FBI had admitted they'd had their eye on Uncle Ron and Jeremy, and had made the connection with Lanier thanks to the RMKU information they'd recently received. When they'd realized Ron and Jeremy were in Montana, they'd come to track them down. Just in time for Chris and Teddy to bring them in.

She made a frozen pizza and sat at her kitchen table to eat. Closing her eyes, she bowed her head. *Lord, I'm very thankful for Your grace today, but I'll still need Your guidance on what to do from here. Amen.*

Lexie knew it was probably safe to return to New

York, and she owed her father an apology for accusing him of embezzling money. Although her father wouldn't be very happy to know that his son and his brother were the real guilty parties. Her parents deserved to know she was alive, not that her being gone had seemed to interrupt their lifestyle. But what they portrayed to the world may be different from what they felt deep inside.

She'd go and make amends. It would be a brief and temporary trip, though. She had absolutely no desire to return to the hustle and bustle of living in New York.

Oddly enough, she'd felt more at home here in Great Falls, Montana. The simple life appealed to her.

Yet the thought of never seeing Chris or Teddy again filled her with sorrow. They'd only known each other for a few days, but the short time they'd been together had changed her. She knew her life would never be the same.

The pizza sat like a rock in her stomach. She pushed away her plate and lowered her head into her hands.

Show me the way, Lord!

Lexie wasn't sure how long she'd been sitting there when she heard a knock at her door. Startled, she jumped up, tipping her chair over in her haste.

Telling herself to calm down, she went over to peer through the window. She'd expected to see Harry, but Chris and Teddy were there.

Hope flared in her heart, but then she realized the pair had probably come to say goodbye.

Chris stood outside Lexie's door, hoping she'd give him a chance. Hours had passed since they'd had to go their separate ways. He'd learned she'd been questioned by the FBI about Jeremy and Ron Hall, while he and Ben filled out reams of paperwork.

When he'd noticed her things were gone from the

motel, he'd panicked at the thought of never seeing her again.

After what seemed like forever, the door opened. "Hi, Chris, Teddy." She smiled and leaned over to pet the dog. "Come in."

"Thanks." His voice was hoarse with nerves. The enticing scent of tomato sauce and cheese hit hard. His stomach rumbled loud enough for Lexie to hear.

"I have plenty of pizza left over if you're hungry."

"Thanks. I didn't stop to eat. I wanted to get here before it was too late."

She tilted her head to eye him curiously. "Too late for what? To say goodbye?"

Goodbye? Was that what she wanted? His earlier hunger vanished. "No, I was hoping for a second chance." He shifted from one foot to the other. Teddy picked up on his nervousness by licking the back of his hand.

"With me? Or with your father?" He grimaced, but she continued. "I think you should consider making amends with your father. I don't see how you can move forward if you don't reconcile the past."

Was that why she'd left him behind at the hangar? He wanted to explain that his feelings for her had nothing to do with his father, but then stopped himself.

She might be right about resolving his past, before moving on to the future.

"Okay, I'll do that right now." He pulled out his phone and scrolled through his contacts until he found the information Ben had sent him several months ago. He decided to use the video chat feature, so they could look each other in the eye.

"Chris?" Drew's face registered shock intermingled with hope. "Is that you?"

"Yes, it's me." He cleared his throat, feeling ridiculously nervous. "I, uh, heard from Ben about your heart issues. How are you feeling?"

"Better now that I'm talking to you." His father's smile dimmed. "I was sorry to hear about your mother's passing."

"Thanks. I didn't know anything about you or Ben until after she died. And I guess I've been carrying around some baggage about that."

"Chris, please believe that if I'd have known about you, I would have taken care of you and Vi." Through the video screen, it was easy to see the regret shimmering from his father's topaz eyes.

The same eyes both he and Ben had inherited, along with the dimpled chin.

"I have to be honest. I'm not sure why she didn't tell you about me."

Drew winced. "I think that was partially the way we broke things off. I'm not proud of what I've done. I was young and foolish. Yet I can't regret the past, not when I hear how much you've accomplished especially within the K-9 unit. And not when I see so much of myself in you."

His throat swelled with emotion, making it impossible to respond.

"Chris, I know you're in Montana, but when you get back, would you stop by for a visit? I'd love the opportunity to learn more about you."

"Of course." This time, he didn't regret the hasty promise. "As soon as I wrap things up here, okay? Just—take care of yourself."

"You, too, son."

Son. The word reverberated through his entire body. After all these years, he had a dad. Their internet connection froze and abruptly disconnected.

"I'm so glad you took this first step in reaching out to your father." Lexie swiped tears from her eyes. "And I appreciate you allowing me to listen in."

"I'm going to do my best to learn how to forgive him and my mother because hanging on to my anger isn't healthy." He hesitated, unwilling to lie to her. "It's not something that's likely to happen overnight, Lexie." He offered a lopsided smile. "I promise with God's help to do my best."

"Chris, that's all I ever wanted," she assured him. She blinked, her eyes bright with tears. "Your mother may have had a good reason to lie to you. At least one that she believed in."

He grimaced. "I know."

"Please, come eat." Lexie reached for his hand, drawing him toward the table.

He tugged on her hand, bringing her closer. "I'd rather kiss you."

Her mouth opened in shock, but she didn't pull away. Or say no. He drew her into his arms, then captured her lips with his.

Lexie melted against him, kissing him back as if she'd never stop. And that was okay with him.

After several long moments, he reluctantly came up for air. Lexie rested her head against his chest, and he was content to simply hold her.

For as long as she wanted.

This was why he'd come back. For Lexie. To have a future. Maybe even a family.

Not that he wanted to rush her into something she'd later regret. For a moment, his failed relationship with Debra flitted through his mind.

He may not know everything about Lexie, but he firmly believed Lexie was the opposite of Debra. Lexie's faith, so similar to his mother's, had drawn him from the very start.

"I plan to attend church services," he said. "The way my mother always did."

Lexie lifted her head to gaze up at him. "You won't regret it."

"No, I won't." He lifted his hand to tuck a strand of her dark silky hair behind her ear. "Would you come with me?"

"Of course," she responded. Then frowned. "You mean, here in Montana? Or where you live in Colorado?"

He hesitated. "Our headquarters is in Denver, but we do travel, quite a bit. To be honest, I don't like the idea of a long-distance relationship. I tried that once. It didn't go well."

"I'm not your old girlfriend," she chided gently.

"You're not anything like Debra, which is a good thing," he hastened to assure her.

She frowned. "Are you really offering to move here, to Montana?"

"You have a plane. You can get me back and forth to Denver easily enough, right?" His teasing smile faded. "The truth is, moving here would mean giving up my job within RMKU, but I'll do that if necessary." He gazed down at her clear green eyes. "Unless you don't want me to?"

"No, that wasn't it," she assured him. "I was actually going to offer to move closer to you. Although, I'm not sure where you live, exactly."

A chuckle rumbled from his chest. "I live in a small house in the suburbs of Denver." He glanced around the interior of her cabin. "But this place has charm, too." His expression turned serious. "I'll do whatever is necessary to stay near you, Lexie. I'd like to see you again, as frequently as possible."

"I'd like that, too. But I don't want you to leave the RMKU, Chris. It's part of who you are."

He cradled her close. "Thank you for that. I enjoy my work. I don't want to scare you or rush you into something you're not ready for, but I want you to know that I've fallen in love with you, Lexie McDaniels. Or Savannah Abigail Hall. Whichever you prefer."

"Lexie," she quickly answered. "I'm not Savannah anymore. I prefer Lexie. And Chris? I think I've fallen in love with you, too."

"I'm so glad." He captured her mouth in another toe-curling kiss. Only when his stomach continued to rumble did he break away. "I guess I should eat."

Lexie stepped back, then offered her hand to Teddy. The dog must have realized she was important to Chris, because his partner licked the back of her hand, too.

"I'll warm up a plate for you," Lexie offered.

"I don't mind cold pizza," he protested.

She ignored him, heating up the pizza and then returning to sit beside him. Chris bowed his head and took Lexie's hand. "Dear Lord, we thank You for bringing us home safely. We ask that You continue to guide us on Your chosen path, and that You help me learn to forgive those who have wronged me. Amen."

"Amen," Lexie echoed.

He took a bite of his pizza, suddenly ravenous.

"I know your brother lives in Colorado, but what about your father?" Lexie asked.

"He lives on a large ranch in Wyoming. Why?"

"I don't have anyone here. Harry plans to sell the hangar and his planes." She shrugged and stole a slice of pepperoni from his pizza. "I think it's better if I move to Colorado."

He stared at her. "Lexie, I would never ask you to do that."

She smiled. "I'm offering, Chris. Family is important. And you'll want to be near Ben and his fiance and daughter. Plus you'll still need time to get to know your father."

"What about your parents?"

"Yeah, I'll have to visit with them at some point, too," she admitted. "But I'm not moving back to New York."

"I'll go with you," he offered. Then he thought about what Ben had told him earlier, about how he and Jamie were planning to get married as soon as possible, for little Barbara June's sake. "Or we can invite them here, for our wedding."

She blinked. "Wedding?"

A smile tugged at the corner of his mouth. He realized that he and his brother were alike in wanting a family of their own as soon as possible. "Yeah, wedding. Lexie, will you please marry me?"

Surprise darkened her eyes, then she smiled brightly, leaning over to kiss him again. "Yes, Chris Fuller. I'd be honored to marry you."

They kissed and hugged for so long, his pizza once again grew cold. But Chris didn't care.

Lexie's love, along with God's grace, was all he needed.

* * * * *

Don't miss Daniella Vargas's story,
Undercover Assignment, *and the rest of the*
Rocky Mountain K-9 Unit series:

Dear Reader,

I hope you enjoyed reading this installment in the Rocky Mountain K-9 Unit series. I had a wonderful time writing Chris and Lexie's story in *Hiding in Montana*. It's always an honor to be included in these continuity stories and I'm very blessed to work with a wonderful team of authors! And we are guided by our fantastic editor, Emily Rodmell.

I adore hearing from my readers! Without you, I wouldn't have any reason to write books. I can be found on Facebook at https://www.facebook.com/LauraScott-Books, on Twitter at https://twitter.com/laurascott-books, on Instagram at https://www.instagram.com/laurascottbooks and through my website at https://www.laurascottbooks.com. You may want to consider signing up for my monthly newsletter, too. Not only will you find out when my new books are available, but I also offer an exclusive novella to all subscribers. This book is not available for sale on any venue.

Until next time,
Laura Scott

LOVE INSPIRED

Stories to uplift and inspire

Fall in love with Love Inspired—
inspirational and uplifting stories of faith
and hope. Find strength and comfort in
the bonds of friendship and community.
Revel in the warmth of possibility and the
promise of new beginnings.

Sign up for the Love Inspired newsletter
at **LoveInspired.com** to be the first
to find out about upcoming titles,
special promotions and exclusive content.

CONNECT WITH US AT:

Facebook.com/LoveInspiredBooks

Twitter.com/LoveInspiredBks

LISOCIAL2021

COMING NEXT MONTH FROM
Love Inspired Suspense

UNDERCOVER ASSIGNMENT
Rocky Mountain K-9 Unit • by Dana Mentink
Innkeeper and single father Sam Kavanaugh suspects someone is
after his three-year-old son—so K-9 officer Daniella Vargas goes
undercover as the little boy's nanny with her protection dog, Zara.
But can they solve the case and its mysterious connection to Sam's
late wife before it's too late?

COLD CASE KILLER PROFILE
Quantico Profilers • by Jessica R. Patch
Searching for the perfect morning landscape to paint leads forensic
artist Brigitte Linsey straight to a dead body—and a narrow escape
from the Sunrise Serial Killer still on the scene. Now that she's the
killer's number one target, partnering with FBI special agent
Duke Jericho might be her only chance at surviving...

FATAL FORENSIC INVESTIGATION
by Darlene L. Turner
While interviewing the Coastline Strangler's only surviving victim,
forensic artist Scarlet Wells is attacked and left with amnesia. Now
she's his next mark and has no choice but to work with constable
Jace Allen to hunt down the killer before he strikes again...

RANCH UNDER SIEGE
by Sommer Smith
Boston-based journalist Madison Burke has two goals when she
heads to the Oklahoma ranch where her father works as a foreman:
heal a family rift...and escape the person targeting her. But when
danger follows her, can Madison rely on ranch owner and former
navy SEAL Briggs Thorpe to keep her alive?

HUNTED IN THE WILDERNESS
by Kellie VanHorn
Framed for murder and corporate espionage, future aerotech
company CEO Haley Whitcombe flees in her plane with evidence
that could clear her name—and is shot out of the sky. Now trapped
in North Cascades National Park, she must work with park ranger
Ezra Dalton to survive the wilderness and assassins.

VANISHED WITHOUT A TRACE
by Sarah Hamaker
Assistant district attorney Henderson Parker just wants to follow
the lead in Twin Oaks, Virginia, to find his missing sister—not team
up with podcaster Elle Updike. But after mysterious thugs make
multiple attacks on his life, trusting Elle and her information might be
his best opportunity to save them all...

LOOK FOR THESE AND OTHER LOVE INSPIRED BOOKS WHEREVER
BOOKS ARE SOLD, INCLUDING MOST BOOKSTORES, SUPERMARKETS,
DISCOUNT STORES AND DRUGSTORES.

LISCNM0522

Get 4 FREE REWARDS!
We'll send you 2 FREE Books plus 2 FREE Mystery Gifts.

FREE
Value Over
$20

Both the **Love Inspired**® and **Love Inspired**® Suspense series feature compelling novels filled with inspirational romance, faith, forgiveness, and hope.

YES! Please send me 2 FREE novels from the Love Inspired or Love Inspired Suspense series and my 2 FREE gifts (gifts are worth about $10 retail). After receiving them, if I don't wish to receive any more books, I can return the shipping statement marked "cancel." If I don't cancel, I will receive 6 brand-new Love Inspired Larger-Print books or Love Inspired Suspense Larger-Print books every month and be billed just $5.99 each in the U.S. or $6.24 each in Canada. That is a savings of at least 17% off the cover price. It's quite a bargain! Shipping and handling is just 50¢ per book in the U.S. and $1.25 per book in Canada.* I understand that accepting the 2 free books and gifts places me under no obligation to buy anything. I can always return a shipment and cancel at any time. The free books and gifts are mine to keep no matter what I decide.

Choose one: ☐ **Love Inspired**
Larger-Print
(122/322 IDN GNWC)

☐ **Love Inspired Suspense**
Larger-Print
(107/307 IDN GNWN)

Name (please print)

Address   Apt. #

City   State/Province   Zip/Postal Code

Email: Please check this box ☐ if you would like to receive newsletters and promotional emails from Harlequin Enterprises ULC and its affiliates. You can unsubscribe anytime.

Mail to the **Harlequin Reader Service:**
IN U.S.A.: P.O. Box 1341, Buffalo, NY 14240-8531
IN CANADA: P.O. Box 603, Fort Erie, Ontario L2A 5X3

Want to try 2 free books from another series! Call 1-800-873-8635 or visit www.ReaderService.com.

*Terms and prices subject to change without notice. Prices do not include sales taxes, which will be charged (if applicable) based on your state or country of residence. Canadian residents will be charged applicable taxes. Offer not valid in Quebec. This offer is limited to one order per household. Books received may not be as shown. Not valid for current subscribers to the Love Inspired or Love Inspired Suspense series. All orders subject to approval. Credit or debit balances in a customer's account(s) may be offset by any other outstanding balance owed by or to the customer. Please allow 4 to 6 weeks for delivery. Offer available while quantities last.

Your Privacy—Your information is being collected by Harlequin Enterprises ULC, operating as Harlequin Reader Service. For a complete summary of the information we collect, how we use this information and to whom it is disclosed, please visit our privacy notice located at corporate.harlequin.com/privacy-notice. From time to time we may also exchange your personal information with reputable third parties. If you wish to opt out of this sharing of your personal information, please visit readerservice.com/consumerschoice or call 1-800-873-8635. **Notice to California Residents**—Under California law, you have specific rights to control and access your data. For more information on these rights and how to exercise them, visit corporate.harlequin.com/california-privacy.

LIRLIS22